RECOLLECTION

RECOLLECTION

GHOST SQUADRON BOOK 6

SARAH NOFFKE
MICHAEL ANDERLE

DISRUPTIVE IMAGINATION®

RECOLLECTION TEAM

INCLUDES

JIT Beta Readers - From all of us, our deepest gratitude!

Dr. James Caplan
Peter Manis
Tim Bischoff
Joshua Ahles
Tim Adams
Sarah Weir
Kelly Bowerman
Kim Boyer
Micky Cocker
Larry Omans

*If we missed anyone, **please** let us know!*

Editor
Jen McDonnell

For Lydia. My greatest treasure in the universe.

-Sarah

To Family, Friends and
Those Who Love
To Read.
May We All Enjoy Grace
To Live the Life We Are
Called.

- Michael

Scowotz, Nexus, Tangki System

The axe spiraled through the air and sunk into the tree trunk, inches from the ogre's face. The tyrant roared, his beady eyes murderous as he glared at the tribe around him. They grunted back, brandishing their axes, ready to throw.

This definitely wasn't the safest place on Nexus, Verdok thought. He'd been searching the planet, trying to determine where Kyra had sent the boy with the mohawk, the last known person to hold the Tangle Thief. Shapeshifting, Verdok had assumed dozens of forms as he searched, and he was no closer than when he started.

The goon that Verdok had been punishing charged away from the tree, his large feet thundering across the forest floor. He pushed both smaller and larger tribe members down as he headed straight for Verdok, an ugly grimace on his flat face.

Smoke from the many fires wafted through the camp, where the primitive race on Scowotz huddled in leather tents or washed their wool clothes in a nearby stream. Verdok, having taken on the appearance of the savage race's leader, sat cross-legged, the black smoke making his eyes burn with irritation. Around him, several of the tribe's males stood, their stance protective. They had no idea that their trusted leader was lying face down in the river, where Verdok had left him.

Those from Nexus, Verdok had found, appeared almost human-like, except they were larger and had distinct differences in their mental and physical capabilities. For instance, this race from Scowotz all had larger heads and poor verbal skills. They were flat footed and nearly toeless, which gave them horrible balance. However, they made up for this with incredible strength and superior height. Even the females were all over six feet tall.

The giant pointed his fat finger in Verdok's direction. "You! Me! Now!"

It had been like this since Verdok had taken on the form of the chief leader. He was constantly tested for his position. They were an ugly race that relied on brutish skills instead of democracy. *No wonder this race is dying off.* Well, also they slept in tents with dirt floors and never bathed.

The putrid smell of the males that charged by Verdok to defend him nearly made him pass out. He picked up the axe closest to him and jumped to a standing position. The chief was easily the largest in the tribe, which was obviously how he'd taken the role. Brandishing the axe over his head, he swung it from side to side, the way he'd seen one of the other males do before battle, obviously an attempt at intimidation. Verdok, as a shapeshifter, was unmatched in his ability to quickly pick up the behaviors of the entity he was impersonating.

The chief's supporters jumped back, hooting deeply. The male who had been about to challenge dropped his chest down, his long arms dangling by his sides and knuckles brushing the ground. The giant grunted, his long hair hanging loosely in his face. Verdok swept his own mop of curly dreadlocks off his shoulders.

This race lived in the overcast north of Nexus for a reason. Their red hair and sensitive skin wouldn't fare well on the southern continents, which Verdok had already searched finding wide open beaches and dark-skinned races who basked in the sun from morning until night.

The savage beat his chest, not at all deterred by Verdok's show of intimidation. Although weapons weren't something he was comfortable with, he'd watched the males of this tribe long enough to know that they never fought fearfully.

When his arm swung around, Verdok let go of the axe and it spiraled through the air, end over end, until it struck the beast in the chest. The giant's thick hands reached for the axe lodged in his torso and froze before they connected with the handle. The crowd fell silent. The tribe members looked around with uncertainty. They grunted to each other, a babbling that grew in intensity as the giant stood frozen, his shocked gaze on the instrument protruding from his chest.

The brute gulped, and blood slipped from the corner of his mouth. This seemed to invigorate the crowd, their grunting growing in volume. The challenger stumbled forward several paces. Verdok didn't move, even when his attacker was close, only five yards away. The beast rocked back on his heels, like he was thinking better of the decision to charge, but then he stepped forward, falling face-first on the axe.

The crowd cheered wildly, many of them throwing their meaty fists into the air. Verdok didn't even grant the fallen tribesman a glance before turning to the rest of his tribe.

"Clear off!" he yelled. "There's work to be done. Get to it!"

The crowd silenced at once, many of them looking at one another like they didn't fully understand the order. Shrugging their enormous shoulders, they slowly dispersed. The men filed back in the direction of their tents, or toward the stream where the females were cleaning and gathering water. The surprise on their faces told Verdok that a leader usually celebrated after a victory when being challenged. However, Verdok didn't care. He was only looking for an excuse to get as far from this primitive tribe as possible. The boy with the black mohawk hadn't been here.

He turned and trudged purposefully in the opposite direction, not even caring that many of the tribe members were giving him curious glances.

When he'd passed through a thicket of trees, Verdok slipped into his original form, enjoying the feel of his own skin. His scales were green and camouflaged into the forest nicely. Once he'd traveled into the cave he'd made his temporary home base, Verdok's mouth began to salivate.

He'd hardly been able to tolerate the charred meat that the females of the Scowotz had offered him. The animal, whatever it was, had been roasted over a hot fire for too long, and the meat had no flavor. He needed something fresh. Something with its blood still flowing.

When Verdok slipped into the cave, the familiar smell of prey filled his nostrils. The firelight danced across the cave walls, but Verdok ignored the nuisance. As a shapeshifter, Verdok adapted easily to his environment, even when not taking on the appearance of another. The Petigrens were warm-blooded animals and needed the fire to survive, especially in this cold region.

Three Petigrens scurried around the open cave, as Verdok slithered into the area and coiled his long tail around his body. They looked up startled, moving backward before correcting themselves and bowing low. Their instinct told them to fear him, but it was their law that told the Petigrens to serve Verdok. A law that the Saverus had created.

"Master! Master!" the Petigrens said in unison between clucking noises. They scurried around, picking up rocks and then dropping them. Digging into satchels while looking around bewildered. The Petigrens were the size of small men, but they had the ears, whiskers and facial features of a mouse. Tufts of hair grew in random places on their faces and body.

"Were you successful?" the first Petigren asked, bringing forward a bowl of fresh water.

Verdok ignored the offering and instead appraised the Petigren. The three had traveled with him for a week now, although when he had set out, he'd had twice the number. He might need more Petigrens soon.

"I was not, unless determining where the boy has not been is considered progress," Verdok said.

Another Petigren rushed forward, sliding down to his knees and bowing his head. "Are you hungry, master? It would be my honor to gather food for you."

Verdok considered the offer. The Petigrens weren't horrible hunters, but usually what they came back with was small and unfulfilling.

"I'll eat in a moment," he said, feeling dirty after his short stint with the disgusting tribe.

"I ventured into the town at the bottom of the mountain," the third Petigren said nonchalantly. Verdok spun around, his yellow eyes widening. "You did what? I told you not to leave the cave."

"I realize that, but I figured I could be of use to you," the Petigren stated, kneeling beside the fire, scratching at the dirt and kindling as though trying to make a bed out of the stuff.

"How did you have such a mistaken notion?" Verdok asked, swaying back and forth, his form stretching tall. Across the cave wall, the shadow of Verdok danced.

The Petigren hiccupped. "I simply went to the village and asked for help."

"You what?" Verdok nearly exploded.

"I said that I needed a safe place, the safest," the Petigren stuttered. The other two were now huddled together by the far wall.

Verdok didn't say anything, instead he watched the Petigren shuffle nervously.

"As a vulnerable race, they didn't question my requests for safety," the Petigren explained, continuing. "And you said that the boy was sent to a safe place."

"I did," Verdok said, revolving to face the other two, who seemed to wet themselves from the eye contact. "Apparently, you don't have a pea-sized brain like your brothers."

"I assure you, we can think when allowed," the rebellious Petigren said, regaining Verdok's attention.

"What did you learn? Or did you only attract unnecessary attention to yourself?" Verdok asked.

The Petigren hiccupped and scuttled forward on all fours before rising to stand in front of Verdok. "I learned that there are many safe places on Nexus. The planet is considered mostly peaceful."

Verdok's forked tongue slipped from his mouth. "That's not helpful. I've garnered that much information over the last several days."

"But I heard rumor of a place considered safer than all the rest," the Petigren stammered, visibly shaking, but still holding his chin upright.

"Go on," Verdok demanded.

"The people in the village said that, for those who pose no threat, the inhabitants of Sunex welcome them into their borders," the Petigren stated, hiccupping still. "They don't allow savages, like those in Scowotz, or other bullies or predator types. However, they will protect those who can't protect themselves. The people are supposed to be very peaceful, and the land absent of any dangers."

Verdok mused on the idea. *That does seem like the safest place on Nexus. Can it possibly be where the hologram sent the kid with the Tangle Thief?*

"Did I do well, Master?" the Petigren asked, not at all cowering now. "Did I prove my worth to you?"

So that was what this Petigren was after? He was trying to prove he was more than a pile of bait or a servant to the Saverus.

Verdok swiveled to face the other Petigren, cowering in the corner. Even shivering in fear, they looked interested to see how this bold behavior would be interpreted. Verdok had to set a precedent. This Petigren's behavior could have far reaching effects. He'd made himself useful by finding valuable information.

Verdok whipped around in a blur and struck the rebellious Petigren, sinking his razor-sharp fangs into the middle of its body. The rat-like man froze, his entire form rigid with fear and adrenaline. He began to convulse in Verdok's wide jaws, which clenched his body tightly, not allowing him to move.

From Verdok's peripheral, he spotted the usual fear from the other Petigrens as they watched one of their kind being struck. But this death served a purpose. The Petigrens were allowed to be mildly useful. They were allowed to sacrifice themselves in battle for the Saverus or to feed the greater species. But they served the Saverus. They did as they were told. What they didn't do was go off on their own and find valuable information that would in turn make them more powerful.

Verdok's body wound tighter around the stiff Petigren, constricting until it was in the perfect position. Then Verdok released his fangs, but kept his jaw wide as he slipped his mouth over the Petigren's head, swallowing it whole.

2

Brig, *Ricky Bobby*, Tangki System

Eddie paced back and forth in front of the bars of the cell. They'd had this area of the brig cleared out of any other prisoners, knowing that was for the best. On the other side of the metal bars, his partner, Commander Julianna Fregin, stared back at him, a doleful expression in her eyes.

"Eddie, how much longer are you going to keep me in here?" Julianna said, her tone seeking to cut him. "I love you, and you've locked me away. What? Are you afraid of me? Are you afraid of my love?"

Unable to control himself, Eddie launched his fist into the wall as he strode the other way. The metal of the ship crunched, caving in from the assault.

"I realize you're angry, but I'm not trying to hurt you," Julianna pleaded.

"Dammit! Shut up!" Eddie yelled, heat rushing to his head.

Julianna covered her face, weeping from behind the cold, metal bars. "Why are you so hostile? All I seem to do is disappoint you. No matter what I do, it doesn't matter."

Eddie gritted his teeth together, pressed his fingers into his palms. *I am stronger than this,* he told himself.

"Tell me what I want to know!" Eddie yelled, his breath hot, spilling over his lips.

Julianna pulled her hands away from her eyes, tears streaming down her red cheeks. She grabbed the bars on either side of her face. "I love you, Eddie. I love you."

Eddie let out a guttural scream, feeling the metal deck reverberate under his feet.

The door to the brig shot open, and Julianna, the real one, stepped through. She halted at the sight of her doppelganger behind the bars, her eyes narrowed. She halted beside Eddie, shaking her head.

"She's fucking crying," Julianna stated. "Please tell me you're not falling for that bullshit."

Eddie pressed his hand to his forehead, shaking his head back and forth. "It's hard not to. It gets into your mind, and you forget what's real and what isn't. This isn't something easy to compute."

Julianna pulled her pistol from her holster and aimed it directly at the Saverus on the other side of the bars.

The monster held up its hands, real fear in its eyes. "You wouldn't shoot yourself, would you?" the Saverus asked.

"Wouldn't I?" Julianna asked matter-of-factly. "You may look like me, but you don't know shit about what I'm capable of."

The Saverus morphed again. It was like looking at a

watercolor painting while on LSD. It took on the form of Eddie.

The imposter blinked back at them, hands up in surrender. "Hey, now. Julianna, you *should* shoot me. I'm not a bad guy, but I'm definitely not a good one."

Julianna lowered her weapon, sighing.

"It's a mindfuck game, Jules," Eddie said, trying to console her. He'd been interrogating the Saverus for an hour and had gotten nowhere. The giant snake kept morphing into different humans it had encountered since being taken aboard *Ricky Bobby*. He and Julianna had really thought that, on the other side of the bars, they could resist the ploy, but it was incredibly tough to look at your partner crying and demand they answer your questions.

Looking as defeated as he felt, Julianna swiveled around to face him. "Maybe we have to give this up for a while."

"Maybe we give it up entirely and throw this monster out the airlock," Eddie said.

The Saverus morphed into the dog figure of Harley, looking up at them with large, brown, begging eyes.

"Fuck, when did it see Harley?" Eddie asked, throwing an arm at the thing.

Julianna let out a weighted sigh. "He was with me when I delivered its food." She pointed to the uneaten tray of roasted chicken and boiled vegetables.

"That's it," Eddie declared. "Only you or I come in or out of here from now on. We don't need it cataloguing others on the ship it can impersonate."

The Saverus shifted into the form of Lars, the only other person it had met, when it woke up on the Q-Ship, before being sedated. "I'm not an 'it'. I'm a 'she'," the Saverus said, using Lars's voice, which made the whole thing even creepier.

"She. Oh, right," Eddie said. "Because I want to ensure that I get your gender correct, you fucking snake."

"As you should," the Saverus said, an entitled tone in her voice that sounded all wrong in Lars's usually humble tongue. "And while you're at it, you should know that I prefer my meat uncooked. And no vegetables."

Now that did sound like Lars, Eddie thought.

"How about we feed you when you start talking? Tell us why the Saverus want the Tangle Thief," Julianna said blankly.

The Saverus shifted into the form of Eddie again. The imposter gripped the bars, pressing Eddie's face between the metal. "I'll tell you anything you want to know, Jules. Anything. But I can't tell you that. Don't you get it? I can't talk. I'm bound by an oath older than you or me."

The real Eddie laughed. "Apparently you don't know how old Jules really is."

"Wait," Julianna stated, staring at the replica of Eddie. "What did you say about an oath? What does that mean?"

Eddie shook his head. "Nothing that imposter says is real. What's the point?"

Julianna didn't look deterred, though. "She slipped up," she said to Eddie before turning her attention back to the Saverus. "You're bound by an oath, is that right? That's why you can't talk?"

"Well, and because she's the fucking enemy," Eddie stated at Julianna's side.

Ignoring him, Julianna said to the Saverus, "Your kind, what they are trying to do, will have horribly devastating effects on our galaxy. If they get ahold of the Tangle Thief, then—"

"*When* they get it," the Saverus said, cutting her off.

"You're not listening," Julianna stated, shaking her head at the form of Eddie.

Julianna turned to the real Eddie. "We need to know more about the Saverus. This is getting us nowhere. There's something preventing this one from telling us anything."

Eddie agreed with a nod. There was something strange about this species, and more than the fact that it could become anything at will. "Maybe Marilla will know."

Julianna turned for the exit, Eddie at her heels. At the door, he turned around and cast a last look at the species that had created more headaches for him than all the alcohol he'd drank in his lifetime. "Just so you know, we will let you rot here. You can't manipulate us. We will figure out how to make you talk."

The Saverus morphed into a version of Julianna and then collapsed. She extended her hands through the bars, sputtering out a cough. "I don't have much longer, Edward," the Saverus said using Julianna's voice, her tone hoarse. "Save me. Please. Don't allow me to die."

Eddie shook his head at the attempt to manipulate his emotions. Although he felt chill wrap around his insides, he pursed his lips.

"Ricky Bobby, you might be the only one safe from this monster," Eddie said to the AI.

"I'll keep a watch on the prisoner, and I'm more than happy to interrogate her when you have new questions," Ricky Bobby said overhead.

This produced a deep scowl on the Saverus's face. An expression he'd never seen so prevalent on the actual Julianna's face.

"That's a good idea, RB," Eddie said, firing his finger at the ceiling. "Thanks."

3

Hatch's Lab, *Ricky Bobby*, Tangki System

"Do you want to work on the DeLorean?" Hatch asked Knox.

The kid looked up from the shelves where he'd been reorganizing loose parts continuously over the last few days. He shrugged, his green eyes full of indifference. "If you want me to."

"Damn it, Gunner," Hatch said, holding a blowtorch in one tentacle and the helmet specifically made to fit his Londil face in another. "The DeLorean isn't like that and you know it. That was supposed to be *our* project. Something we did away from all the demands of Ghost Squadron."

Knox's gaze drifted over to the far corner, where his father had set up a small workstation. "Maybe my dad will want to help you with the project."

Hatch had the urge to throw the blowtorch, but he knew that was a dangerous impulse that he must quell.

"Cheng isn't a mechanic, and you damn well know it. He's a scientist."

Knox dropped a bolt into one of the container units and shrugged apathetically. "You used to work together, though."

"Yes, and he took care of the science end of projects while I handled mechanics," Hatch explained.

"So?" Knox's voice sounded so unlike him, all of his normal respect absent.

"So, with you, I'm able to focus on the science, because your mind is naturally wired for mechanics." Hatch paused, waiting for Knox's defeated expression to disappear. When it didn't, he added, "It's a nice balance. Better than what Cheng and I had, and look at what we were able to accomplish."

"Yeah, you created a device that tears the universe apart, and I lost it," Knox said, his voice sounding dead. "Like I said, you need a different apprentice."

Hatch suppressed the urge to scream. He couldn't fault the boy, not really. It was tough when someone you cared about was going through a major loss. Hatch wanted to tell him that things would get better and that experience told him that these things would pass. Instead he said, "And I don't need a new apprentice. I'm not allowing you to quit on me, Gunner."

"Fine, but I don't think you should allow me on the current project," Knox stated.

He isn't looking for sympathy, it occurred to Hatch. *He fears himself.*

Knox didn't scare Hatch, though. He respected the hell

out of the kid. Somehow, at the young age of ten, Knox had operated the Tangle Thief, which was impressive in itself. However, he had the sense to hide the dangerous device, figuring that bad guys were after it; unfortunately, he hid it so well that no one could find it, not even him.

"You aren't getting out of working on the Saverus goggles," Hatch said, shaking his head before he fitted his helmet into place. "Now hand me that damn blood sample and quit sulking."

Knox's eyes shot to the vial of blood from the Saverus they had imprisoned in the brig, which Julianna had delivered to them.

"I don't have all damn day, kid!"

Hatch didn't like having to yell at Gunner, but someone had to shake him up and tell him to stop being a baby. That's what he'd told his own kids growing up. Now they were off on their own and doing great things, hopefully because Hatch didn't coddle them.

Knox handed over the blood sample, a bit of interest in his gaze. "You're using an aluminum alloy for the goggles?"

Hatch's eyes glanced at the goggles on his workstation, the prototype he'd created that would hopefully spot a shapeshifted Saverus. "Yeah, what of it?"

Knox shrugged, a gesture he was doing a lot lately. "No reason."

"Oh, you asked, but have zero reason for the question. Yeah, that makes sense," Hatch said, his tone dripping with sarcasm.

"Well, I get that the aluminum is lightweight, but due to the chemistry of the goggles, I'd think that something like a titanium alloy would be better." Again the kid shrugged. "But what do I know?"

Hatch peered at the prototype, his mind sifting through all the relevant data. Then he picked up the goggles and dropped them in the garbage.

"Gunner, you know a hell of a lot more than you give yourself credit for. That's why I need your help, but you're going to have to get your head back in this game."

Gaping at the trashcan where the goggles now sat, Knox shook his head. "You're starting over?"

Hatch shook his head, pulling his helmet down in front of his face. "Hell no. *We're* starting over. Now put on your welding mask."

"Uhhh…all right," Knox said, and some of the heaviness was gone from his voice.

Hatch had started the welding torch, when he heard someone calling his name from behind.

"Doctor A'Din Hatcherik!" a voice yelled.

Hatch switched off the torch and spun around. "What? What? What do you want?!" he fired. He pulled up the mask and immediately sank back an inch.

Liesel Magner stared at him apologetically, holding a pad in her hands. She was wearing her usual getup, yoga pants, a loose, off-the-shoulder sweater, and, curiously, the new/old chief engineer also wore charger cables in her short blonde hair. Each day, she seemed to have some electronic or mechanical part incorporated into her outfit.

He found this highly annoying. They were parts, not fashion accessories.

"Sorry to interrupt you, but I wanted to have you

review a new set of plans that I've drafted," Liesel said, offering the pad to Hatch.

The ferret, Sebastian, climbed down from Liesel's back and disappeared into the spare parts storage. That's where both the ferret and Knox spent most of their time lately.

Hatch puffed out his cheeks, looking disinterested. "What's this for? The gate drives?"

Liesel shook her head. "I've already got the gate drives up and ready to go. Your instructions were helpful, and Ricky Bobby was a tremendous help."

"Thank you, Liesel," Ricky Bobby chimed in from overhead. "I'm glad that I could contribute."

Hatch felt a tension in between his eyebrows. "Well, they can't be up to Federation specs. I'll fix that once I'm done here."

Liesel smiled, showing a row of perfectly straight, white teeth. "No need. When I say they are ready to go, I mean they are up to Federation standards. We're ready to gate whenever needed."

"Oh, well, I'm sure you think so," Hatch said, sounding not at all convinced. "Even still, I'll check the drives before our next gate attempt."

"I assure you that's not necessary," Ricky Bobby irritatingly broke in. "I've tested the drives, and everything is in order."

Hatch pinned two of his tentacles to his side and grimaced. "I haven't experienced a gate, so it's impossible that you've tested them."

"It's a computer simulation I've constructed," Ricky

Bobby stated. "I can upload all physical changes into the model of the ship and then test different situations."

Liesel's perky smile widened. "Isn't that brilliant? That's how we could determine the best possible way to upgrade the existing gate drives. It took much less time than it should have."

Hatch grumbled to himself, turning back to his workstation. He'd picked Liesel himself, and yet this all irritated him. He'd wanted the best, but she was too good. And more irritating than that, she was...cute. Hatch respected Julie because she was competent and strong; Liesel was that, but she was also...something else that threatened him somehow.

"Doctor A'Din Hatcherik?" Liesel asked at his back.

Pretending to already be engrossed in his work, Hatch looked up like he didn't expect to find her there. "Huh? What?"

"The plans I drafted for an upgrade," Liesel asked, handing him a pad. "I was hoping that you'd review them and give me your thoughts."

Hatch reluctantly took the pad from her. What he found was not what he expected. "You can't be serious?"

Liesel giggled. "I know it seems a bit..."

"Aggressive," Hatch filled in the word that she was struggling to find.

"Yes," she agreed with a nod. "I had the privilege to sit down with Jack Renfro and review the types of missions that Ghost Squadron has undertaken in the past. That's where I got the idea for this project. It's extreme, but I'd trust this kind of technology with the captain and commander. I believe they wouldn't abuse it."

"You refused to install nukes in this ship under Felix Castile's command," Hatch argued.

"Yes, because Felix was a man who would abuse such technology," Liesel countered. "Jack expressed his concern that *Ricky Bobby* is ahead in speed and stealth, but lacks proper defense."

"That's why we need rail guns and mains," Hatch said, shaking his head at the chief engineer.

"I don't disagree, but apparently, we're a little way off from securing that kind of ammunition," Liesel said.

"And you think you have the capability to do something like this?" Hatch pointed with his tentacle at the pad.

Liesel reached down when Sebastian returned from the supplies area, a mischievous look on the ferret's face. "It's fairly straightforward. I mean, think of it this way, you may not be able to make a volcano, but all you need is vinegar and baking soda to create an explosion."

Hatch threw up four of his tentacles, aghast. "Can you believe this?" he asked Knox. "She thinks she can make a weapon with baking soda and vinegar."

Knox had taken the pad from Hatch and reviewed the plans. He looked up, a quizzical expression on his face. "Actually, the logic is sound, here. She's not using lava to make a volcano—or a weapon, in this case. She's using something much less sinister, but it will have similar results. It's actually pretty smart, and would be incredibly helpful in a pinch."

"'In a pinch'?" Hatch asked in disbelief. "Like if we

wanted to level a city block? When did that become our call?"

"We're the good guys," Liesel said, smiling as she took the pad back from Knox. "What about when the Brotherhood were trying to take over that small continent on Nexus? Wouldn't it have been helpful then to immobilize their forces?"

Hatch shook his head. "We don't kill the innocent."

"Right," Liesel agreed, folding her arms across her chest, thinking. "Well, how about when that ammunition supply needed to be destroyed on that moon?"

"We jumped next to it and achieved fine results," Hatch reminded her.

"From reviewing the notes, it appeared that Ghost Squadron took out the whole moon, when just a small section comprised the ammunition area," Liesel countered, which made Hatch's head suddenly hot.

"All I'm saying is this would be a precise, honed attack that Ricky Bobby could employ in a pinch," Liesel concluded. "Just because we have bombs or bullets doesn't mean we have to use them."

"Yeah, I guess I can see the relevance," Hatch said reluctantly. "Fine. I give my permission for the project."

"I don't believe that Liesel was looking for permission," Ricky Bobby stated overhead. "As chief engineer, a position that you approved her for, she is neither higher or lower than you in rank."

Liesel's face flushed pink. "Thanks, Ricky," she said, looking embarrassed. "Honestly, having your blessing would be great. I wanted you to see the plans to endorse their effectiveness."

Hatch turned away from the engineer, hiding his own flushed face. "Yeah, fine. It all looks okay. But if it's a complete screw-up, then I'm not a part of it."

"Fair enough," Liesel said. "Thank you, Doctor A'Din Hatcherik."

Hatch waited until Liesel's retreating footsteps faded away and then he turned for the back of his lab. His head wasn't in the current project anymore.

"Let's take a break," he said to Knox. "Shall we work on the '69 Corvette Stingray, or the 67 GTO?"

"Uhhh... whatever you want, Doc," Knox said, treading carefully. He could sense Hatch's new sour mood.

"Okay, Stingray it is, then," Hatch stated, waddling over to the supplies area. His mouth fell open, and he had to stop himself from screaming.

"Gunner, what did you do here?"

The area was completely and revoltingly organized. All the bolts, screws, and other parts were each in their respective bins.

Knox joined him, and his own mouth fell open. "Doc, I promise. I didn't do this. It must have been..."

Hatch narrowed his eyes. "That damn ferret."

4

Bridge, *Ricky Bobby*, Tangki System

Finally! How long have I been tracking the Otterbots?

He'd lost track.

Jack Renfro tore around the corner, nearly running into the new Chief Engineer on his way to the Bridge.

"Sorry," he said as Liesel stumbled back, her pad falling from her hand. It clattered to the floor, falling face down.

Jack stooped to pick up the fallen pad, knocking heads with Liesel as he did.

She backed up, rubbing her head. "Ouch."

"Double sorry," Jack said, grimacing. One of the jumper cables Liesel wore in her hair had knocked him in the temple.

"It's okay," she said, readjusting the small, red cable she'd used to pull her hair back on one side. "I think I got you worse than you got me."

Jack massaged his temple, opening his jaw to clear away some of the tension. "Well, you are wearing metal in your hair," he joked. The young engineer was dressed in stretchy black pants and a cream-colored sweater. She had a pirate's smile, and a look in her eyes like she'd remembered a joke.

Liesel's eyes drifted up in the direction of her hairline. "A bit unorthodox, I know. My friends say I'm eccentric for the sake of being different."

Jack laughed. "That sounds like something only a friend could tell you." He looked down at his crisp, button-up shirt and slacks. Jack had never known what it meant to be eccentric; he preferred his own appearance to be a bit more polished.

"Good news," Liesel said, pinning a bit of blonde hair behind one ear.

Jack's thoughts darted to the Otterbots, and he wondered how he'd forgotten about them. Time was critical. "What's that?" he asked, his pulse quickening.

"Hatch signed off on the plans," Liesel said, turning the pad over and checking the screen, thankfully still intact.

"Hatch. Yes, that's right," Jack said as another idea related to the Otterbot mission sprang to his mind.

"You look like you've got something demanding your attention," Liesel observed.

Jack blanched at the astute comment. "Actually, I do. Thanks for the update. I've got to get to the bridge."

He took off at a sprint, careful not to run into any more crew members as he passed.

"Think about it," Eddie encouraged. "That's all I'm saying."

"I've already thought about it, and the answer is no," Julianna said, turning her attention to the fast-approaching footsteps at her back.

Jack rounded the corner a moment later. The welt on the side of his head was the first thing the others saw.

"What happened to you?" Eddie asked Jack, when he stopped, breathless and nearly doubling over in front of them.

"What?" Jack asked, looking down at his clothes.

"Are you bleeding?" Julianna asked, staring at the wound on the side of his head.

He wiped his hands across the cut and eyed his wet fingers. "Oh, it's nothing. I bumped into an eccentric." Jack smeared the blood on a pristinely white handkerchief he'd pulled from his pocket.

"Oh, so Liesel, then?" Eddie guessed.

It wasn't a risky guess, since there was no one quite like the chief engineer on the ship. She could be found in the morning meditating on the observation deck, and had asked Ricky Bobby to announce that she'd be holding "yoga retreats" in the evening.

Julianna felt bad because she was pretty sure these extracurricular activities weren't going to have any attendance.

Maybe you should join her, then, Pip offered in Julianna's head.

Yoga isn't really my thing.

You should keep an open mind, Pip said with a laugh.

Ha-ha.

"I have urgent news," Jack said, stuffing the bloody handkerchief into his pocket.

Julianna shot a tentative expression at Eddie, who returned it, his gaze instantly worried.

"Is it the Saverus? Has she gotten away?" Eddie asked in a rush.

Jack shook his head. They'd discussed the security complications with imprisoning the alien on the ship. "No. It's something much more pressing," Jack began. "For years, the Federation has been trying to track down a group that was known to occupy a territory on the Frontier. We haven't been able to find their headquarters, but I believe we've intercepted a signal from one of their ships headed to their base, which is in Federation territory. Ricky Bobby believes the transmission was supposed to be scrambled, but he's gotten better at picking up and deciphering these."

"That's great!" Eddie said, a look of zealous excitement immediately springing into his eyes.

"I'm guessing Ricky Bobby has a tracker on the ship, then?" Julianna asked.

Jack nodded. "Yes, but you're going to have to go after them quickly. They are headed toward Ronin airspace."

"Ronin? Wow. They have been hiding under our noses. We can be on their tail in no time," Julianna stated.

She looked around, assessing who was in the general vicinity. Lars and Fletcher bolted to attention at once, striding over. Having an alert team that was ready to spring into action with a single glance was something she appreciated immensely.

"The quicker, the better," Jack replied. "However, this is

a dangerous group; if they sense they're being followed, we'll miss our chance to find their home base. For that reason, I just want you two to take one Q-Ship. Having the element of surprise would be best, and mobilizing the ground forces quickly is too much of a risk."

"Why don't we organize our forces and attack when we learn where the headquarters are?" Eddie asked.

Jack shook his head. "That probably won't work. Following in behind them is key. We've been trying to find the Otters' headquarters for quite some time. I'm guessing to get in there, we need special clearance, which I'm hoping you can get by sneaking in behind this rogue ship."

Eddie pursed his lips and nodded. "That makes sense. Tip-toe in behind these guys before they have a chance to shut the door, so to speak."

"Exactly," Jack said, motioning to Julianna and Eddie. "I want you two to go in there and execute a swift strike."

"What about Fletcher?" Eddie asked. "Wouldn't it be better to have some backup?"

"No," Jack said at once, looking at the lieutenant. "As talented as you are, I don't think it's a good idea to be in close proximity to the Otters. They are too dangerous."

"Is this when you tell us who these Otters are?" Eddie asked.

Jack glanced at his watch, taking a steadying breath. "They are a group of assassins who have been eluding us for too long. This is our chance to take them out. They only take jobs outside of the Federation, but left unchecked, they could become a huge problem."

"Yeah the last thing we need is assassins wandering into federation space," Julianna said adamantly.

"I agree. I'm happy to be on the team that exterminates these killers," Fletcher said, standing taller next to Eddie.

The stubborn look on Jack's face deepened. "These aren't your run of the mill assassins. They are incredibly powerful, with a strength that will even challenge the captain and commander."

"What?" Eddie asked. "You said they've operated outside of the Federation all this time. How did they get enhancements?"

Jack laughed humorlessly. "They *are* enhanced, but not in the same way as you and Julianna. The Otters, or 'Otterbots', as they are also known, are cyborgs."

"Oh, fuck," Eddie said, whistling through his teeth. "I haven't seen a cyborg in…well, I can't even remember how long it's been."

"And these cyborgs operate as a group of assassins for hire?" Julianna asked.

"Yes, and although we know they've been employed mostly on the Frontier, this ship we're tracking is headed to Ronin, which could be where their headquarters are located," Jack explained.

So they don't live in Otter space? Pip asked, his tone completely serious.

His perfect delivery caused an abrupt laugh to escape Julianna's mouth. All three men looked at her, curious expressions on their faces. She waved them off.

"Sorry. Pip is making bad jokes in my head, as usual."

Eddie gave her a look of jealousy. "Sounds like it was a pretty good joke, actually."

Julianna shook her head. "Okay, we'd better head out. Ricky Bobby, you still have a lock on the Otters' ship?"

"Yes, and I've run simulations based on the ship's continued trajectory, and have a rough idea of where they are headed to on Ronin," Ricky Bobby informed.

"Damn, that's one smart AI," Eddie said.

Tell the captain that I take unintended offense to that, Pip sang.

You can tell him yourself when we're in the Q-Ship, Julianna said.

Yes, I can tell him all sorts of things.

Don't you even think about it, Julianna warned.

I'm thinking about it...

"Lars. Fletcher," Jack called when the two were about to turn. "I have a mission for you, as well."

"Yes, sir," Fletcher said, rolling his shoulders back and giving Jack his full attention.

"I need you, Lars, to fly a Q-Ship to Ronin, separately from the commander and the captain." Jack looked at Fletcher. "And I need you to accompany Knox on that ship."

"Oh, Ronin..." Fletcher said, realization dawning on him.

"Knox's home planet," Jack nodded. "I'm thinking that, since we're so close we might as well take this opportunity.

Maybe visiting Knox's childhood home might jog his memory with the Tangle Thief."

"But you're worried that it could be a trap?" Fletcher asked.

With a reluctant nod, Jack said, "That's why I want you there. We shouldn't draw much attention to your presence so I want it to be an in and out job. However, I know that the Saverus are on the hunt for information on the Tangle Thief, and they might also have thought to retrace Knox's footsteps."

"Not to mention that they will want to get their hands on the boy," Fletcher said, a crease marking his brow.

"No matter what, you can't allow that to happen," Jack insisted. "I'm not saying that because Knox is the only one who knows where the Tangle Thief is. He's a part of our team. Don't allow anything to happen to him."

Fletcher saluted. "I'll protect him with my life."

5

Alpha-line Q-Ships, _Ricky Bobby_, Behemoth System

Eddie hadn't stopped laughing since the Q-Ship had flown out of the launch tube to follow the Otters' ship.

"Are you done?" Julianna asked while locking onto the target, a one-person ship that the Black Eagles could do loops around. Although the Q-Ship was cloaked, they kept a safe distance as the rusty ship neared Ronin airspace.

"That's some funny shit," Eddie said through a laugh.

"See," Pip urged overhead, "the captain gets my humor."

"'Otter space'," Eddie repeated yet again, slapping his leg.

"If I was interfaced with the captain, like I am with the Q-Ship and you, Jules, then we'd all be one, big, happy family," Pip declared.

"No," Julianna barked.

Eddie observed how high her shoulders were pinned; she tensed every time they talked about this possibility. He didn't know what the hang-up was, and she hadn't been any closer to sharing it with him.

"Okay, okay," Pip started. "I've got a joke."

"No!" Julianna yelled, her face flushing red.

"Maybe it's a bad time," Eddie said, stifling his own laughter.

"Why did the big otter make a small fire?" Pip asked, ignoring Julianna's sour mood.

Silence.

Pip gave a fake cough.

Eddie darted his eyes sideways at Julianna, and resigned himself slightly. "Go ahead, Pip. Why did the big otter make a small fire?"

"Because he wanted to be a little h-h-h-otter!" Pip's laughter filled the cockpit.

Eddie couldn't help himself, and joined in. The joke was so dumb, he liked it.

Julianna rolled her eyes, initiating the thrusters as the ship ahead of them sped up, passing into Ronin's atmosphere. "That's the worst joke ever."

"Fine, I've got another one," Pip said through seemingly unending laughter. "Where do otters keep their money?"

Julianna looked straight at Eddie, her face stone. "Don't you answer that. Actually, ignore him completely."

Eddie's face broke, and the wide grin he'd been suppressing sprang free. "Oh, come on. Even you have to admit that one's funny. Of course otters keep their money in river banks."

"Yahoo!" Pip sang. "We have a winner!"

Eddie wanted to reach out and shake Julianna by the

shoulders. One moment she was his best friend, his partner, and then the next, she'd walled herself off from him. It was happening more rapidly lately, like she was afraid of something. But apparently talking about it was definitely out of the question.

"Can we focus?" Julianna asked over Pip's continued chuckles.

Through what sounded like a wheezing breath, Pip said, "Yes, of course. I otter be ashamed of myself." He burst into renewed laughter.

Eddie cleared his throat, trying to sound unaffected. "I wonder what's up with the name 'Otter' for these cyborgs."

"That's a good question," Julianna said, relaxing a little. Talking business always put her at ease.

"I can answer that," Pip imparted, his tone suddenly neutral. "Jack didn't have a chance to brief you entirely on the Otterbots, since the discovery of this ship was unexpected."

"Go on, then," Julianna urged.

"I'll tell you. I promise," Pip paused, "after one more joke."

"Pip, we're almost there," Julianna complained, leveling the Q-Ship out and following the Otterbot vehicle.

Its body was much slimmer than a Black Eagle's, and had impressive fluidity, although it wasn't as fast. The hatch for the cockpit was oversized, which made its contents even more curious.

"What's the difference between a pizza and an otter?" Pip asked.

Eddie eyed Julianna, who pretended to not have heard Pip, then asked, "What's the difference?"

"A pizza doesn't scream when you put it in the oven," Pip answered.

"Oh, fuck," Julianna said in a hush, giving Eddie a pointed stare.

"Yeah, even I must admit, Pip, that's a bad otter joke," Eddie stated.

"Well, what can I say, I guess we're *drifting* apart," Pip said and howled again with laughter.

"Okay, now tell us, what's the deal behind the name 'otter'?" Julianna asked.

"The name was originally given to these cyborgs as a derogatory joke by the Trid," Pip explained. "As cyborgs, they were seen as lesser and usually referred to as mutants. No one took them seriously, since they are only half-human or half-Trid."

"Some of the cyborgs are Trid?" Eddie asked.

"They came out of the research facility on Kai," Pip said.

"You mean, Pistris Station, where Jules risked her life to save bunnies?" Eddie asked, scowling at her.

"Move on with your life, Teach," she said at once.

"Yes, Pistris was where these cyborgs came from," Pip continued.

"It makes sense that those shark-fuckers would name their pet projects 'otters'," Eddie stated.

"Otters who became assassins. Shit just got weird," Julianna said, shaking her head.

"None of them have any otter DNA, in case you're

wondering," Pip said. "Three are human, and three are Trid. According to the files, they escaped from the facility a few years ago. Later, the Federation got wind that the six had formed an assassin team. Besides taking out their original creators, they've also targeted many higher-ups in the Trid government."

"Which is why the Federation allowed them to exist for this long," Eddie deduced.

"Well, if they were taking out the Trid, then they were probably doing us a favor," Julianna qualified.

"Exactly," Pip said. "But they've gone unchecked for too long, and their targets are getting closer to the Federation."

"It's only a matter of time before they come after one of our own," Eddie said, growing anxious for the fight to come.

"So they took on the name their creator gave them as a joke?" Julianna asked, sounding perplexed.

"Oppression and bullying is a great motivator," Pip answered. "Their name is a constant reminder of the wrongdoing that started their journey."

Julianna set the Q-Ship down behind the Otterbots' vehicle. This area of Ronin looked like the rest of the planet: rundown and filled with industrial pollution. It was hard to make out much through the smog that glowed orange around them. The ship had halted in the middle of a barren wasteland littered with wreckage.

Eddie thought that the ship must be lost and rechecking its maps, but then a large, metal door rolled back from the ground to reveal a huge chasm.

"Think we found our assassins' evil lair," Eddie said, leaning forward. The ship in front of them moved forward working its way through the opening and underground.

Julianna didn't hesitate, speeding into the space where the ship had been and lowering into the large shaft, following undetected in the cloaked Q-Ship.

"Oh, and one more thing," Pip said, that familiar teasing tone in his voice.

Eddie tensed, preparing himself for what bomb the AI would drop.

"The Otterbots, much like the sea creatures they are named for, prefer the frigid cold," Pip explained.

"So it's going to be as cold as fuck in the facility, is that right?" Eddie asked, his eyes rolling back in his head as he clenched his fists.

"Bingo," Pip said. "They are machines; they wouldn't want to overheat."

Alpha-line Q-Ships, Saddal City, Ronin, Behemoth System

"Feels good to be in the co-pilot seat, doesn't it?" Lars had asked Knox as he'd flown them to Ronin.

Knox had offered his friend a shaky smile, but hadn't answered otherwise.

If he had, he would have said that nothing felt good anymore. Not working on the cars or tinkering with the new projects or even flying.

Lars didn't need Knox's help flying the Q-Ship, but he'd asked for it to make Knox feel better.

That was the thing, though. Everyone wanted something from him lately, and it was overwhelming. They wanted him to feel better. To recover his memory. To remember what he'd done with the Tangle Thief.

What if I let them down?

"I think they're waiting for you," Lars said, still in the pilot's seat, conducting post-flight checks. He indicated the back, where Knox's father and Hatch were pretending like they were confused—for five minutes, they'd been debating whether the old house was the one on the right or the left.

Thanks to the cloaking technology of the Q-Ship, Lars had set it down in the shabby overgrown yard that stretched in front of the abandoned houses. Knox knew which house was his. Maybe his father really didn't remember, since his mind hadn't been the same after the Tangle Thief, but it was more likely that Hatch and his father were waiting for Knox to wake up and join them for the mission that he'd been brought here for.

"Yeah, I know," Knox told Lars, and peeled himself out of the seat, giving his friend one last uncomfortable look.

"Hey," Lars called when Knox had started for the back of the ship.

"Yeah?"

"It's not easy to return home," the pilot said softly.

Lars knew some of what Knox was going through. Lars had to return to Kezza when he thought that he'd never see his family again. Although their past was different, Lars could still relate.

"Yeah, it feels weird," Knox admitted.

"That's because whatever you think you'll find in there," Lars pointed through the window to the dilapidated house across the yard, "is a part of who you *used* to be."

Knox swallowed, rubbing his calloused fingers together. "I guess I don't understand why that would make me feel strange."

Lars offered Knox a rare smile. It looked odd on the Kezzin's usually serious face. "It seems to me that you've spent a lot of time looking forward. Maybe it's tough for you to look back."

Knox's chest tightened. He shrugged to try and cover the sensation. "Yeah, maybe."

"I bet you wouldn't ever look back, if you didn't have a good reason," Lars said honestly.

"Yeah, if only the galaxy's future didn't depend on me." Knox laughed morbidly.

Lars didn't join him. Instead he continued checking the gauges, his interest suddenly back on his work. "Sometimes, Knox, the universe gives us gentle nudges. I'm guessing that you've ignored those."

"So I'm getting pushed, is that it?"

"If we're all connected, then fighting our personal demons is as important as fighting the biggest bad guy out there."

Knox turned his back on his friend, irritated by what Lars probably thought was sage advice. He knew he was trying to help, but Knox wasn't in a place where he knew how to accept advice.

Fletcher ducked his head around the open door. "I've swept the whole block. All is clear. You ready?"

No, Knox thought stubbornly. But he forced the corners of his mouth up and faked a smile. "Yeah, sure thing," he lied.

6

Alpha-line Q-Ship, Landash City, Ronin, Behemoth System

The Q-Ship hovered in place before turning one hundred and eighty degrees so Julianna could spot the Otterbots' ship. The rusty vehicle had dropped straight down before parking against the far wall of a large underground warehouse. Dim lights showed that the room was cluttered with equipment around the perimeter. Five single-person flyers sat in a line where the landing ship had parked.

"Assassins are fucking filthy pigs," Eddie observed.

"Well they are worse than pirates, so I can't say I'm surprised," Julianna stated.

"You think so? Pirates are the lowest of the low, I thought."

"Pirates kill others for their riches," Julianna reasoned. "But assassins kill others for someone else's money."

Eddie nodded. "Yeah, I never understood how someone

could take a blind order to kill. I'm no saint, but at least every fucker I've blotted out deserved it. I know that with certainty."

Julianna gave him a skeptical look. "What about that one guy at that bar that got in the way?"

Eddie shrank back with a confused look, but quickly recovered, shaking his head. "Don't fuck with me. That never happened. I don't miss a target and hit the innocent."

Julianna smiled to herself. "You haven't missed yet, Teach. *Yet.*"

Taking out six cyborgs assassins wasn't going to be easy, but Jack had been right to send only Eddie and Julianna. This could get ugly fast. Storming these guys wouldn't have been the right strategy; assassins reacted too fast for such an approach. Instead stealth would be Eddie and Julianna's best advantage. Oh, and being fucking badass.

Julianna secured her armor before checking her weapons. She had a pistol strapped to each leg, a set of sheathed blades on her hip, a round of Hatch-perfected grenades in her pocket, and a rifle in hand.

When she looked up, Eddie was giving her a curious expression. "What?" she asked.

"I think you have room for another weapon," he said.

She shook her head at him. "I wish I had the tri-rifle."

"I seem to remember you got that amazing weapon blown up," he teased.

"It was you, Teach, and you damn well know it," Julianna said, trying to make her voice sound threatening.

Eddie slid up to the door for the Q-Ship. He glanced

over his shoulder at Julianna. "Ever notice that you slip between calling me 'Teach' and 'Eddie'?"

Julianna shrugged. "No, why?"

"Just think it's curious," he said coyly before opening the hatch door.

Saddal City, Ronin, Behemoth System

Knox was the last one to step into the boarded-up house. He kept expecting something to rattle around inside of him, but he mostly felt numb. Surprisingly, the house didn't look much different than he remembered. It had been plain to begin with. Now the peeling paint and dust-covered surfaces only made it look like a washed-up memory that belonged to someone else.

A hand clapped him on the shoulder. Unhurried, he turned to find his father staring at him with watery eyes. "How are you doing, son?"

Knox's mouth fell open, but he simply shrugged.

His father offered him a tender smile. "It's a lot to process. It's been over ten years since you've been here. Be gentle with yourself."

"Or…" Hatch said, drawing out the word, "push yourself to remember what your subconscious is trying to hide."

"Hatch," Cheng said in a protective tone.

"The boy is tortured," Hatch said, waving a tentacle in their direction. "The sooner he remembers what happened to the Tangle Thief, the sooner he can be done with this."

Knox couldn't help smiling at Hatch's practical nature.

The Londil definitely didn't sugarcoat a damn thing. Maybe that's why Knox had preferred his attention more than his own father's lately. After ten years of separation, one might think that father and son would long to catchup. But when Cheng looked at Knox, his eyes were haunted by regret.

"I need a minute," Knox finally said, setting off in the direction of his old bedroom.

It was the first door on the left, right next to his father's room. The workshop was in the back; Eddie and Julianna had told him that he'd disappeared from that room. It was where the receiver for the Tangle Thief had been located.

Why don't I remember any of this?

The door to his old room squeaked mercilessly as it opened. The room, which he actually remembered, was fairly clean. Action figures stood on a shelf on the far wall. A chest full of building blocks and loose parts sat next to a lumpy bed. The memories didn't rush back. *What was I expecting?*

"I remember that you used to rummage through my trash bins in my workshop," Cheng's voice said behind him.

Knox turned to find his father framed in the doorway.

Cheng pointed to the chest. "That's where you'd keep all the parts I'd thrown out."

"Oh," Knox replied, not sure what else to say.

Cheng strode farther into the room, stopping in front of the chest and peering down at it. "I used to tell you that it was trash, and that's why it was in the rubbish bin."

"Yeah, I remember that," Knox said, pushing his hands

into his jean pockets. This didn't just feel weird anymore. It felt *wrong*. Like he'd broken into a stranger's house with a stranger in place of his father.

Cheng turned, giving Knox a pained smile. "Do you know, I started throwing out perfectly good parts just so you'd have something useful to tinker with?"

Knox's heart palpitated suddenly. "You did? That's weird."

Unabashed, Cheng shrugged. He squatted down, opening the chest. "Maybe it seems a little strange. I just always thought that you'd go on to do something great if I gave you the right tools."

"Little did you know that I'd go on to lose the tool," Knox said morosely. He knew this self-defeating attitude was doing him no good; he was starting to get on his own nerves. But it was hard to stop abusing himself, now that he'd started.

Cheng held up a mess of wires and bolts. "What was this, anyway?"

Knox nearly choked on the spit in his mouth. The memories blasted him like an assault rifle. The walls within his mind that had prevented him seeing his past came crashing down. The dust cleared showing him what had eluded him.

He used to pretend to make whatever project his father was making. The object his father held up was *Knox's* version of a Tangle Thief. He remembered that he'd been holding the other part of it when he left his room. He remembered! Memories were rushing back to him.

He saw clearly in his mind the day his father disappeared. Knox had opened the door to his bedroom. The living room was empty.

"Dad?" he'd called out, his crummy version of the Tangle Thief in his hands.

Guessing his father was in his workshop as usual, Knox headed in that direction.

The memories were clear now, like photographs that had recently been taken.

He remembered walking into the workshop... His father wasn't there, but part of the Tangle Thief was. And it was glowing. Knox wasn't scared. He'd been trying to find his father all day, using his own Tangle Thief, but of course it hadn't worked.

Knowing that this was his best chance, Knox reached out and grabbed the glowing Tangle Thief his father had left behind. With the receiver in his hands, he operated it the way he'd seen his father do when configuring the settings.

Knox whipped his head up, an urgency in his eyes.

"What is it?" Cheng asked, sensing the immediacy in his son.

Knox didn't answer. Instead, he spun around and sprinted out of the room, through the living area, and into the workshop.

Hatch looked up at Knox's sudden entrance, and Knox's eyes fell to a burned section in the middle of the floor. That was the last place he'd stood.

Hatch indicated to the spot with his tentacle. "A tear was opened right there it seems, probably after you were transported, and definitely after we'd searched the house for you two. Thankfully it appears to have closed naturally, but this is an example of the repercussions of using the Tangle Thief."

"Are we in danger?" Knox asked, staring around the old workshop.

"Radiation levels appear to be normal," Hatch reported. "A few years ago, they were probably lethal."

"And every time the Tangle Thief is used, it will open one of the tears in the universe?" Knox asked, even though he already knew the answer. He was talking because it was easier than facing the truth.

"Yes, as you damn well know, the Tangle Thief creates tears when used. And these tears will get larger and larger, as it is used more often and for bigger jobs," Hatch said, waddling over until he was standing right in front of Knox. "Now, you want to tell me why you're staring at that spot?"

Knox pulled his gaze away from the floor, not quite looking at Hatch. "It all came back to me. I remembered everything that happened. I remembered using the Tangle Thief to find my father."

"You did?" Cheng asked at Knox's back.

He couldn't bear to turn around and face his father, so he continued staring at the floor.

"But...?" Hatch asked.

"But..." Knox covered his head with his hands. "But after entering Area 126, I can't remember anything else."

7

Landash City, Ronin, Behemoth System

Brodie ran the polishing rag over the hilt of his katana, his attention momentarily distracted as Dec's ship landed.

It's about damn time, Brodie thought.

He'd been on watch for most of the night and was fucking tired as hell. The metal on metal in his spine crunched as he stood from his station by the entrance to the Otterbots' headquarters. He picked up the raccoon hat he loved almost as much as his sword, and stuck it on his head.

The katana had been a gift from his father, who didn't know that the same steel would be operating his son's body one day. Because of the damn Trid scientists, he was currently seventy percent machine. They had said that he should be happy to be alive. Then they'd laughed at him and called him 'Rabid Raccoon' and a 'dysfunctional otter'.

Those scientists hadn't been laughing when Brodie lopped their heads off with a single stroke of his sword.

The hat, which was starting to lose some of the hair on the tail, had been a gift from his grandfather. He used to tell Brodie stories of raccoons tearing through his garbage back on Earth. His grandfather had tried time and time again to catch the creatures, but they'd always foiled him. 'Trash pandas', he'd called them.

His grandfather learned the animals were attracted to metal. He fashioned his own version of a bear trap, right out in the open with no bait in it. The racoons' own curiosity got the better of them, and it was one such unlucky animal whose fur made Brodie's hat. He somehow related to the animal, as strange as it was to admit. His own attraction to metal had been both his undoing and his saving grace.

Brodie slipped his father's sword into the scabbard at his back as Dec lumbered around the ship. The obnoxious Trid wore a crooked smile across his face that was flecked with blood. *So the mission was successful, it appears.*

Dec's lower half was titanium, which meant that he made a shit-ton of racket when trotting to his bunk at night. His shark face was completely intact, which was too bad because there was nothing good about the pointy nose or black eyes.

Brodie still couldn't believe he'd partnered with a Trid, but the money was good, so who cared if they killed a few targets to stay alive?

It was about survival of the fittest, and they were the strongest around.

"Hope we're having steak, because I damn well deserve it," Dec yelled, shouldering his giant gun.

Brodie was opening his mouth to tell the fucker off when, almost silently, three bullets ripped into Dec, the last one going through his head. Dec stumbled forward, blood bursting from the wound on his head, before he fell.

Behind Dec stood two figures. A tall man with a fierce expression who held a rifle, and a defiant woman, her hands calmly by her side.

These fuckers picked the wrong place to raid, Brodie thought, pulling his sword and. whipping it up sharply, swinging it through the air in a blur.

The man fired his rifle, but sharp movements of the katana easily deflected the bullets. This wasn't Brodie's first rodeo; if these two fucktards were raccoons, they'd make great hats after he was done with them.

Brodie halted when the firing ceased, and lunged low, his sword positioned in front of his body. The man lowered his weapon, giving his partner a look.

"Shoot him in the foot," she ordered.

Is this chick serious? His foot, like most of the rest of him, was pure steel. He smiled, gripping the hilt of his sword. He wouldn't even have to deflect the next attack.

The man lowered his weapon slightly and shot three times at Brodie's foot. The assaults had no effect on him, and the man reloaded his gun. Brodie was preparing to launch forward and take these pirates out for good, when the woman reached for something.

It was all a blur. Brodie had been focused on the man and staring at his own foot. He didn't notice the woman pull out a blade and launch it through the air until it was too late. It spiraled closer and closer until it stabbed him in his fleshy chest.

He gurgled on a mouthful of blood. Then he stumbled back, hit the wall, and choked on his last breath.

"'Shoot him in the foot'?" Eddie asked, kneeling down to retrieve the knife from the cyborg's chest. He wiped it on the dead man's sleeve before handing it over.

"It was a diversion tactic," she said, taking the knife and sheathing it. "I had to inflate his confidence, otherwise we were never getting past that damn sword."

"Speaking of the sword," Eddie said, looking down at the dead man. "What do you think of adding it to our personal collection? I kind of like the idea of slicing that baby through the air."

"It's not a fucking rail gun, but sure, why not," Julianna conceded.

"What is he wearing on his head?" Eddie asked, inspecting the strange hat with a striped tail hanging from its side.

"It's made from a raccoon," Julianna explained. "This guy apparently thought he was Davy Crockett."

"Who is that?" Eddie asked. The name sparked something small in the back of his mind.

"The Alamo. Texas Revolution," Julianna supplied.

Eddie shook his head, nothing coming to mind.

"Are you still reading Alice's Adventures in Wonderland?" she asked.

"I've moved on, actually," Eddie admitted. "Chester has me reading the Hobbit now."

"Alright, no more fantasy for a while," Julianna said with a smile. "You're brushing up on history."

"You and Chester handle my reading list, would you? I've got enough to think about," Eddie said, sliding his ear up to the door where the raccoon cyborg had been stationed. On the other side, Eddie could make out booming voices.

"Remember to aim for the fleshy parts," Julianna said, hiding a sneaky grin.

Eddie readied his weapon. "Unless we want to inflate their ego, and then we shoot them in the foot."

"Exactly," Julianna said, picking up her boot and slamming it into the closed door.

Two Trids and one man bolted upright when Julianna busted through the door. The closest one, a Trid with a metal face and one red, glowing eye, launched himself at them. He was all brute force, and not even a little nimble, with grinding gears moving his limbs.

The other two searched the room, obviously trying to locate their weapons.

Let them find them. It will be more fun that way, Julianna thought.

I'm sensing a weird signal from the next room, Pip informed her.

You think it's our last cyborg?

I think that whatever it is, you'd better be careful.

You telling me to be careful is worrisome.

Firstly, focus on these guys who apparently have metal plates obstructing their reasoning.

Pip was right. Julianna had merely lurched to the side when the cyborg Trid raced at her. His head had busted through the wall, where he was now pinned, trying to get unstuck.

Julianna whipped around and swept the Trid's legs from underneath him. The fucking metal bit into her leg and hurt like a bitch, but she successfully took him down. He sputtered out several choking sounds as he tried to regain his balance.

Eddie had abandoned the guns, which was probably a good idea, since ricocheting bullets was a real possibility with three cyborgs in the room. He fended off attacks from both sides, as the man whipped his metal fist at him while the Trid brandished a bo staff.

Julianna yanked the trapped Trid out of the hole by the back of his shirt, the wall ripping open his throat. Blood gushed from the giant laceration and started to form a pool beneath the Otterbot.

The other cyborgs looked up, shock on their faces. Julianna guessed that it wasn't every day that two puny humans walked in and bested these guys.

They both glared at her with white-hot anger.

"Oops," she said, dropping the Trid to the ground.

The man flexed his fists, the hydraulics in his joints making a sharp sound.

"Oh, did you want to play?" Julianna asked, holding up her purely human knuckles.

She liked everyone, whether they were part machine or not, but she fucking hated murderers. That wasn't what Ghost Squadron was; she'd never thought of soldiers on the battlefield that way. They were defenders of justice. Protectors. Those willing to sacrifice themselves for the greater good. *These* men were fucking cowards who preyed on individuals because they couldn't look themselves in the mirror.

Eddie looked to be humoring the Trid, jumping back out of the way as the bo staff nearly sliced him in half. Julianna wanted to laugh.

The man in a steel suit, the one with only one red eye, held up his giant fist. The knuckles spiraled like the top half of a rubik's cube until a small cannon surfaced.

Fuck, I should have seen that coming.

I was so expecting it.

Shut the fuck up, Pip!

The end of the cannon glowed orange—a sure sign that it was ready to fire.

Without guns as a viable option, Julianna set off at a sprint. She launched off a chair sitting to the side of her, ricocheted with one foot off the nearby wall, and leapt for the man. Before he could react, her legs wrapped around his head, and she yanked back, dragging him to the floor.

The metal man fell hard, his weight crushing Julianna. She managed to roll out from underneath him before he could scramble up, giving her the advantage, but she didn't know what do with it. His entire back was a complicated mess of metal wires, and he was pushing himself up, although his cannon was making it difficult. She heard the gears as his body shifted, working the cannon back into his hand.

Press a knife in between the space along his armor at the base of his neck, Pip said, his voice urgent.

Huh. I don't think I can.

This cyborg was covered in sheaths of metal, unlike the raccoon man they'd taken out.

All cyborgs have a weak spot. His has to be between the armor. That's your best option.

Julianna pulled out a knife and, with lightning force, drove the blade down. She expected it to meet metal, which at first it did, but then it slipped between the sheets of armor and sliced deeper into a texture she recognized.

Flesh.

The cyborg collapsed, the lights extinguished and the noisy gears stopped grinding.

Thanks.

No problem. I've always got your back.

Julianna looked up to find Eddie standing in front of the cyborg Trid, who had his own bo staff protruding from his chest.

Eddie turned, appraising the kill Julianna had made. "Just gotta find their soft spot, huh?"

Julianna grimaced. *Between you and Eddie, I get my fair share of bad jokes.*

Although I'd prefer to follow that up with a pun, I need to draw your attention to something.

Julianna tensed at the sudden serious tone of Pip's voice. *What?*

Whatever is on the other side of that door over there...it just got a lot more intense.

By 'intense', do you mean angry?

I don't know what I mean. This isn't something I recognize.

So we should probably storm in right away then?

Definitely. Ask questions later.

Eddie readjusted his armor and steadied his weapon. Fighting the Trid cyborg had nearly made him break a fucking sweat. If the assassin wasn't pinned to a wall with his own staff, Eddie would have told him off for such a thing.

He was about to laugh to himself when he caught the serious expression on Julianna's face. Well, more serious than usual. Actually, in battle, she looked half giddy. A trait he appreciated about her.

"What's up?" he asked.

"Pip is concerned about what's on the other side," Julianna said, motioning to the door.

"Like that it's mostly machine and has a grasp like a vice grip?" Eddie asked.

"He's not sure," Julianna said. "But doesn't it appear that it wants us to come to it?"

Eddie stared around at the dead cyborgs. "We did make enough noise to rouse everyone on Ronin."

"My thoughts exactly," Julianna stated, worry in her tone.

"Is it a trap?" Eddie asked.

"Even if it is, what do we do?"

Eddie stared between the closed door and Julianna. "We can't turn back now. We're supposed to take them all out."

"Right, which means we're going in."

Eddie stepped in front of her. "Of course we're going in. But I'm going first."

Exactly as Julianna had done when they entered this room, Eddie lifted his foot and slammed it through the metal door. It busted almost completely off the hinges and hung sideways.

The room on the other side was filled with smoke, like an explosion had occurred. In the overhead lights, Eddie could barely make out debris littering the space. Food wrappers and packing material were everywhere. He kicked it out of his path as he marched forward.

His boot crunched down on a can, and he looked to find something that filled him with disgust. A fucking Pepsi can. Of all the things to find. It made him hate these cyborgs more.

A cough marked by screeching metal caught his attention. Eddie looked up to find mostly spiraling smoke, but then it began to clear and a figure materialized on the other side of the room.

Like the other cyborgs, this one's body was predominantly covered in armor. However, the man, only fifteen feet away, was smaller than the others. Tubes ran from his armor into the top of his head, making him look like some sort of prehistoric sea creature.

His eyes glowed red.

Eddie lifted his weapon, searching for the right place to aim. The smoke cleared suddenly, like being sucked into a vacuum. Then a screeching sound filled Eddie's head, so loudly he doubled over with pain.

Unable to hold onto his rifle, he dropped it. His head and the searing pain inside was all he could give focus to. A bomb had detonated in his skull, and his brain felt close to exploding. He was only marginally aware of Julianna down on the ground beside him.

Whatever that cyborg was, whatever he could do, he was taking them both down without even moving.

Julianna tried to scream, but nothing came out. She strained to recapture control of her limbs, but with her brain on fire, she was lost.

It felt as though her head was being forced through a sieve. The figure in front of them stood casually, watching with his glowing red eyes.

Julianna, she heard over the crushing pain that sounded like a forest fire in her mind.

Her mouth parted, and she made to say, "What?" but nothing came out.

Julianna, Pip's voice came again.

Drool puddled under her face, which was pressed to the ground. The pain was too heavy for her to hold herself up.

Julianna, I can help you. But you're going to have to turn your thoughts over to me.

She couldn't process that. She couldn't think. The blinding, scorching pain was all she could feel.

Julianna! Let me have control of your thoughts. Then I can block out the cyborg.

I don't know how.

He's in your mind. Causing this pain.

I know!

Just grant me full access. Turn it over to me. You'll still have control, but I need a chance to put up a firewall.

But how?

Pretend to go to sleep.

How could she sleep when the aching, throbbing torture was robbing every moment of her sanity?

Let go, Pip urged.

Julianna tried to pull in a conscious breath, and snot trickled down out of one nostril. She was losing control. It was only a matter of time before her heart stopped beating.

Let me have control. It's as easy as handing me the key.

Julianna didn't know what that meant. She *did* know what it felt like to surrender, though. With the blaring pain still overwhelming her, Julianna pretended as if this were a battlefield and it was time to surrender. She acquiesced with her last bit of remaining strength, her eyes falling shut, and the world going black.

Fuck. This better work.

Pip was frantic. This was a chance. A risk. But Julianna had done what he'd asked—she'd turned her mind over to him. Now he had to hold up his end of the deal. Save her life.

No biggie.

Her heart rate is dropping. Oxygen levels are on the decline.

Focus, Pip.

Stop talking to yourself.

Stop telling me what to do.

There it is! There's the firewall for Julianna's consciousness. If I can just reinforce it, then I can shove this fucking cyborg all the way out.

Oh, fucking shit. Blood pressure plummeting. No! No! No!

Don't you quit on me, Julianna Fregin. I've nearly gotten that trespasser out of your brain. I just need ten more seconds to reinforce perimeters. Firewall will be impenetrable in five, four, three, two...

Wake up!

Julianna felt like she was drowning.

Wake up already.

Her head cramped as she pushed drool away from her mouth. She didn't realize she was sitting back on her heels until her eyes opened to find the smoky room.

Oh, good, you've decided to fucking join me.

Julianna still couldn't remember where she was or why a red-eyed robot was staring at her. She did recognize the voice in her head, though, as if it were her own.

Pip, when did you start cursing?

Since you decided you could take a nap on me and nearly die.

Die? Julianna looked around. Eddie was sprawled out beside her. *Oh, fuck! That cyborg.*

Yes, and he's going to turn Teach's brain to pudding unless you stop him. I have the firewall protecting you, but there's nothing I can do for the captain.

But I don't know how to kill this one. He appears to be mostly metal. How am I going to find the weak spot?

He doesn't appear to be the physical type, so why don't you just leave him here and run the fuck away?

You know I can't do that. However, that does give me an idea.

She dug into her pocket furiously. Testing her limbs, she jumped to a standing position and darted for Eddie. He was pale and looked like he was suffering worse than she had.

Damn it, he's almost gone.

Because I can't guard him the same way I can you.

I get the point. We will discuss this sharing you business later, once I've saved Eddie's ass.

Julianna lifted Eddie up with ease, securing him on her shoulder. He started to convulse.

The cyborg is trying to kill him. You have to get him out of here.

Julianna knew Pip was right; they didn't have a moment to spare. Taking off at a sprint, she didn't even worry that she was dragging Eddie's legs. They bumped over the trash and fallen cyborgs in the other room. When Julianna was almost out of the second area, she pulled the clip from the "holy" hand grenade Hatch had given her and launched it back, straight through the door and into the room where the red-eyed cyborg was.

She darted forward, continuing on. The blast knocked both her and Eddie into a wall, but she didn't stop. Distance was key. When they were almost to the Q-Ship, she realized that Eddie's feet were underneath him, and he was ambling forward, like a drunk man being led to bed.

"Eddie, are you alright?" she asked.

He picked up his head, but kept his eyes shut. "Yeah, but I feel like I've been shot in the head."

That sounds about right, Julianna thought.

I've uncloaked the Q-Ship and it's ready for departure.

Thanks.

The cyborg appears to be offline now.

So it's dead? Julianna asked as she loaded Eddie's mostly limp form into the back of the ship.

Yes, I don't think it could have survived that blast.

That cyborg was an evil motherfucker.

Agreed.

And he'd have killed both of us if not for you.

If that's your way of saying 'thank you', then you're very welcome.

Julianna slipped into the pilot's seat, letting out a weighty breath. *That's my way of saying I have a lot to think about.*

Like that I should share a place in both your head and the captain's?

Julianna cloaked the ship, lifting it into the air and up to the door they'd come through.

We will discuss it later. For now, open the gate to this place, or Hatch will have my ass for banging up his ship.

Already done. I've hacked into their security system. You're good to go.

8

Intelligence Center, *Ricky Bobby*, Behemoth System

"I'm sorry, but I don't get it," Marilla said, leaning over Chester's shoulder and eyeing his screen.

An exaggerated sigh fell out of his mouth. "It's easy. You make your character get a job. You have to feed and socialize them and take care of their basic needs."

"But why?" Marilla asked.

Chester moved the cursor and made his sim sit down and watch TV. "Because it's fun. You know, that emotion that makes you happy?"

Marilla straightened, shaking her head. "I don't see the point in playing a video game that simulates real life. Why not live life?"

Chester paused his game and spun around to face her. "That's boring. And there's many benefits to playing a game of this sort."

A challenging look sprang to Marilla's face, and her brown eyes narrowed. "Do indulge me, Mr. Wilkerson."

Chester held up a single finger. "For starters, playing the Sims helps to calm our brain and feed our need to have control over our life." He leaned forward, looking around with mock caution. "Don't tell anyone, but we actually have little control; it's all an illusion."

"Not only does none of that make sense, but you're totally making it up." Despite her attempt at skepticism, Chester spied the laugh Marilla was hiding.

It was Chester's turn to give Marilla a look of utter offense. "I do not spout lies nor am I one of those pesky people who pretend to know things or make them up as I go. This universe, sweet, naïve Mar, isn't a system that we control."

"How do you know that?" She stood back, crossing her arms in front of her chest.

"Simple. I study the codes that string this universe together."

Marilla flashed him a mutinous expression. "You're a hacker."

"Bingo. And who better to understand how the universe is striving for chaos rather than organization than a hacker?"

"Chester, I'm usually open to many things you try and lecture me on, but—"

A startled gasp fell out of Chester's mouth. "How dare you? I don't lecture you."

Harley trotted over, interested in the heated exchange that was only half-bordering on joking.

"As an anthropologist, I—" Marilla began.

"You want to believe that there's meaning to all this,"

Chester said, cutting her off again. "You want to hope that there's a cosmic purpose that we're all building toward."

"I do believe that." Marilla threw her arm out indicating the room at large. "How can you be a part of Ghost Squadron and not know that?"

How did an instructional lesson on a video game turn into a philosophical argument? Chester probably should have seen this coming. This wasn't really about God or life or purpose. Usually the smaller underlying things fed these much larger diatribes. Strange, but true.

"Mar, do you really think that one day our job on Ghost Squadron will be done?" Chester paused, waiting for her answer. When there wasn't one, he said, "Because I don't. There will always be a bad guy to fight or a terrorist to stop. That's because the universe doesn't strive for perfection, but rather chaos and disorder."

"That's a very pessimistic perspective to have," Marilla said, leaning down to pet Harley, but looking like she was the one who needed the reassurance.

"Chester is most likely correct," Ricky Bobby chimed overhead.

The scowl on Marilla's face deepened. "What? Ricky Bobby, how can you say that?"

"In my research, I've found that systems that are left alone gradually devolve into disorder," Ricky Bobby stated matter-of-factly. "Nothing in this universe is certain except entropy."

"Nice word," Chester said with a big smile. Entropy was exactly how he defined life. Everything was constantly moving toward a disarranged state.

"Are you saying that the only certainty in life is that there isn't any?" Marilla asked, a new ache in her voice.

"I'm saying," Ricky Bobby began, "that all systems break down, and we're constantly combating entropy. The only certainty in life is that we're in a constant state of change. From my research, I've deduced that the purpose in life is to try and do everything we can to combat this eventual degradation through acts of survival."

Chester clapped once and held his arms out wide. "Which perfectly explains how the Sims video game mirrors our own life, and therefore has value."

"You've spent over thirty-six hours playing that game in the last few months," Ricky Bobby said. "I can only deduce that it is a drain on your productivity and possibly on your creativity."

Chester's mouth popped open. "I would implore you, good sir, to mind your own damn business."

He'd expected that this jab would bring a smile to Marilla's face, but she didn't even look close to grinning. Her eyes were brimming with tears as she chewed on her lip.

"Hey, Mar," Chester said, softening. "It's all theory. Life is what you make it."

She nodded, but didn't look entirely convinced.

"Life is more complicated than that, but currently there's something else more pressing," Ricky Bobby stated.

"What's that?" Chester asked.

"I believe it will be brought to your attention in a moment," Ricky Bobby replied.

Chester and Marilla shared a bemused expression. "The

big guy in the sky loves mystery. He can't simply tell us what's going on; I, of course, am referring to Ricky Bobby, if you were confused."

Marilla sniffed, a fragile expression lingering in her eyes.

Chester was about to say something comforting—that was obviously bullshit, by his standards—like 'everything is going to be alright', when he was interrupted by a banging noise. As Harley barked wildly, Chester looked up, as he usually did when waxing with Ricky Bobby. "I'm guessing that's the interruption you were alluding to."

"You are correct," Ricky Bobby replied.

With a sideways look at Marilla, Chester took off for the far wall. A loud bang reverberated from behind the wall before it popped out completely. Liesel stumbled out, falling on the metal panel as it crumpled to the deck.

"Are you alright?" Marilla asked, stooping down to help Liesel up.

Chester peered into the cramped vent space from where Liesel had emerged. It was a dark mess of wires and tubes, and two beady eyes stared at him from up high. Chester shrank back, directing his attention at Liesel.

She had grease smeared on both of her cheeks, and her hair was matted to her head.

"What were you doing in there?" he asked her.

Letting out a breath, Liesel smiled. "I was rewiring the Intelligence Center. I think it's up to your specs now."

Chester peered back into the chasm. "You already finished the rewiring job? By yourself?"

Liesel laughed. "Don't be silly. I had help." She clicked

her tongue twice, and the beady-eyed animal scurried down a series of tubes until it was on the ground, the ferret that was usually on Liesel's shoulder.

"Sebastian helped you with the wiring?" Marilla asked in awe.

"Of course," Liesel said with another laugh. "You don't think I could have fit into those tiny places and have done all the work myself do you? That's mad."

Chester popped his head into the inside of the ship for a third time. "Yeah, Mar, completely mad. What were you thinking? Obviously Liesel had a ferret helping her." He pointed to Harley, who was eyeing Sebastian hungrily. "I'm thinking of teaching Harley here code so that I can be that much more productive."

"Cutting back on your video game time is probably the most viable option to increase productivity," Ricky Bobby cut in.

"Thanks, Rick Bob, but again, your observations aren't welcome here," Chester stated, winking at Marilla.

Liesel brushed off her pants. "I couldn't help overhearing your conversation regarding the universe and, well, the purpose of life."

"Because you were inside the walls of the ship?" Chester asked playfully.

"I promise I don't eavesdrop regularly," Liesel said with an apologetic smile. "Next time, I'll tell you all when I'm working on your area."

"Or better yet, have the mongoose tell us," Chester said.

Liesel turned to Marilla offering her a sensitive look. "Although I think that Ricky Bobby and Chester make some valid points, they don't entirely line up with my thinking on the matter."

"It's hard to argue with an AI," Marilla said, her tone dry.

"That's true, but even Ricky Bobby is not a supreme source of knowledge," Liesel stated. "For what it's worth, my own inner journey to discover the outer world has taught me something entirely different than the points they were trying to make."

"What's that?" Marilla asked, hope springing to her eyes. Chester liked that expression on her; it was the one she wore most days when talking of her work. Marilla was usually full of wonder and reverence for the world, rather than discouraged by it like she was now.

"It's true that we are constantly moving in the direction of death," Liesel began. "I can't argue with that. All stars must burn out; it's inevitable. But they burn for a reason. The fact that they are progressing toward an end shouldn't undermine that they exist in the first place. Isn't it the finite aspect of life that gives it purpose? In a way, I think our constant progression toward death is an attempt by the universe to conspire for our own good."

"I'm not sure that Zen business makes any sense," Chester argued.

"It's all about perspective," Liesel said with a smile that reached up to her blue eyes. "You think there's no purpose. That there's nothing out there. That life is an eventual path to destruction, right?"

"Through the walls of the ship and huddled around

parts and wires, you can hear perfectly fine, I see," Chester said.

"I simply believe that even if we are headed toward nothing, that the path is still meaningful." Liesel shifted her gaze to Marilla. "That's what worried you before, right? That we're here for no reason and going nowhere?"

Marilla nodded. "It's a cold possibility. I've studied hundreds of races. How can it be that there's no meaning to it all?"

"Because maybe we're not as important as we like to think we are," Chester argued. "We could be a speck on the tip of a pencil, for all we know."

"You and Ricky Bobby believe that there's no certainty in life, and that our only purpose is to preserve ourselves as long as possible, correct?" Liesel asked.

"I liked the way Ricky Bobby put it better, but yes," Chester said.

"And you, Liesel, believe something different?" Marilla asked.

"She has faith," Chester interjected. "You believe there's a bigger purpose, a cosmos connecting us all."

"I might," Liesel said brandishing one of her pirate smiles.

"Well, sweetheart, there's nothing to prove that you're right," Chester said.

"And the same goes for you," Liesel fired back. "There's no way to prove the absence of something. But I can prove that we have a bit more control than you think."

"How's that?" Chester challenged.

"Well, even if we're headed for death, our path is inside our control," Liesel said.

Chester pushed his glasses up on his nose. "I'll argue that you're wrong."

"Because everything is random, in your opinion?" Liesel asked.

"I pretty much rule the Dark Web, so I'll argue that my opinion holds a bit more weight than others," Chester said with a laugh.

"I have a method that will prove to you that there's a symmetry to life. There's a synchronization that connects us all and proves that there's meaning to our lives," Liesel said.

"Prove away, then." Chester pushed his arms out wide, exaggerating the movement for effect.

His overstated movement knocked a can of pens to the ground, and the sudden commotion spooked Sebastian, and the ferret streaked out of the path of the falling objects and through Liesel's legs, sprinting for the exit. Harley whipped around and ran after the ferret, barking.

"Sebastian!" Liesel called, running out of the Intelligence Center and after the racing animals.

9

Jack Renfro's Office, *Ricky Bobby*, Behemoth System

Toweling off after a ten-mile run, Jack checked himself out in the mirror. His parents told him that obesity ran in their family and may be unavoidable. He'd politely told them that was a self-fulfilling prophecy. At thirty-six, he was in the best shape of his life.

"You are one handsome fellow," he said to his reflection.

"I like to call you a sexy motherfucker," Eddie said from the open door.

Jack laughed, waving Eddie and Julianna into the office. "You caught me doing my mirror talk. ArchAngel used to make fun of me when I did it."

"What does Ricky Bobby say?" Julianna asked.

"I think that it's perfectly normal, and a positive way to maintain a healthy self-image," Ricky Bobby stated.

"So that shows how much ArchAngel knew," Jack said, fanning his sweaty shirt. He couldn't admit that he missed the old ship or its AI. In truth, he didn't think that he missed *her*. He was more aware now of the space she had filled in his life. ArchAngel nagged him constantly and teased him about his odd behaviors. That wasn't companionship, but he might have mistaken it for that.

"You'll have to excuse my appearance," Jack said, wiping sweat off his forehead. "I just got a lead I've been tracking, and needed to relay the information to you two straight away."

"Are you sending us after more Otter assassins?" Eddie asked with a laugh.

"Or to a planet where we're ambushed by porcupine catapults?" Julianna asked with mock seriousness.

Eddie gave her a look of awe. "Good one, Jules."

"I stole it from Pip," she admitted.

"Damn, that AI is sharp," Eddie observed.

"He's something," Julianna stated, a heavy look on her face.

"No, this mission doesn't include any hostile animals, that I know of," Jack said with a chuckle. "Good job, by the way. The general told me to pass along his sincere gratitude for taking out those assassins. He wanted to tell you himself—credit you all for erasing the threat—but as you know, this is not a glory squadron."

Eddie nodded. "We do it for the sheer thrill of knocking out bad guys."

"I know you do." Jack screwed the lid off a water bottle and downed a quarter of it, wiping the back of his hand across his mouth. "The job I have for you should be fairly straightforward. I've been successful at locating a psychiatrist on Onyx Station."

Eddie turned to Julianna, his smile dropping. "Oh no. We're having a mental intervention. I guess it is overdue."

Jack should have seen that joke coming. He shook his head. "Not for you two. Dr. Bennett Harrison specializes in hypnosis and is the very best."

"For Knox?" Julianna asked.

"Precisely." Jack downed the rest of the water. "The memories around the Tangle Thief are locked away in his subconscious. I'm confident that this psychiatrist can get them out."

"Great!" Eddie said excitedly. "We take the kid to the doctor, and then we can patronize a few bars on Onyx Station."

"Actually, I suspect that it's not going to be as easy as you think. There's still a minor complication," Jack said.

Eddie let out an impatient sigh. "Right. Of course, there's some sort of snag to this. What's wrong with this doctor? Is he an angry cyborg? Protected by thuggish Trid?"

Jack threw the empty water bottle across the room, where it bounced off the trash can and landed on the floor. "No, nothing like that. As far as I know, Dr. Harrison isn't dangerous at all."

"Well, the suspense is absolutely killing me. Do tell," Eddie said.

"Oh, is that right?" Julianna asked Eddie before glancing at Jack. "In that case, take...your...time." She drew out the last few words, breaking them into multiple syllables.

Eddie busted out with a laugh. "Damn, Fregin is on a comedic roll today. Is that one of Pip's jokes too?"

Julianna scoffed. "I've got my own material."

Jack couldn't help laughing at the partners. They'd come a long way since they first started working together.

Stifling a grin, Julianna said, "So what's up with this psychiatrist?"

"He thinks he's a bird." Jack lowered his gaze, pinching his nose and awaiting the response.

"You can never just send us to a normal person for a normal job?" Eddie asked, his tone amused.

"You'd get bored so fast, and you know it," Jack replied.

"True," Eddie chirped.

"A bird? This psychiatrist, who is the best in hypnosis in the galaxy, thinks he's a bird?" Julianna asked.

"Well, it depends on the day, actually." Jack strode over to his desk, retrieving the file on Dr. Harrison. "The doctor has an unclassified mental disorder. Strangely, he's been under evaluation for years, and they can't determine what exactly is wrong with him. He displays symptoms for schizophrenia, dementia, OCD, bipolarity, and a half dozen others. It's been quite perplexing to the staff of doctors who oversee his care."

"Isn't there someone else you can send us to?" Julianna asked.

Jack handed her the file. "I'm afraid not. Dr. Harrison is not only the best, but he's also the best choice for this particular job. As a patient of the mental ward on Onyx Station, he won't be sharing this sensitive information with anyone; which is perfect, since we need the information surrounding the Tangle Thief to remain quiet. If anyone finds out that the device is floating around out there, we'll have more than the Saverus interested in finding it."

"I thought doctor-client privilege was a thing," Eddie stated.

"I think we all know that those rules can be broken," Jack said. "I don't trust this information with any ordinary psychiatrist."

"So you're sending us to a crazy one," Eddie said with a laugh.

Julianna was about to ask another question about this Dr. Harrison, when loud barking distracted her. The sound of racing feet echoed from the hallway. Julianna turned in time to catch Sebastian speeding by, quickly followed by Harley. The ferret made a hard turn, scurrying into the office.

Julianna jumped back as the two animals sped past the group. Sebastian climbed up the floor lamp in the corner, jumped onto a painting, and traversed to the top of the frame. From there, he squeezed through the slats of a vent and disappeared. Harley barked once more before turning tail and running out of the room.

Liesel halted in the doorway, looking around. "Sebastian? Have you seen him?"

Julianna pointed to the vent. "He went in there."

Liesel leaned over, hands on her knees as she heaved on ragged breaths. "Oh good. He got away from Harley."

"Well, to be fair, Harley still looks to be on the hunt," Eddie said.

Liesel waved him off. "If Sebastian is in the vent system, he'll make a straight shot for my personal quarters."

"That's one smart ferret," Eddie stated.

"Let's see if he's smart enough to fix some of the holes in the ventilation system while he's in there," Liesel said with a laugh, straightening up.

"I didn't see him with his toolbox when he ran by, so probably not," Julianna joked. She was in a more humorous mood today for some reason. It must have been the near-death experience with the mind-fucking cyborg. Not quite biting the bullet always put her in a good mood.

Liesel strode farther into the office and picked up the empty water bottle that Jack had thrown. "Plastic water bottles really aren't good for the universe."

Jack reached out and took the bottle from Liesel with an apologetic smile. "I realize that. I was in a hurry and grabbed one."

"I get it," Liesel said with a wink. "Sorry, I can be a real nag sometimes."

"No, no." Jack crunched up the water bottle and deposited it in the trashcan. "And sorry about my appearance. I just finished a run."

"What's with the apology, Jack?" Eddie asked. "You pretty much told *us* to deal with your sweaty clothes."

Jack's eyes darted in Eddie's direction, and Julianna could have sworn there was a punishing look in his gaze.

"Running is good, but can be damaging on the knees," Liesel said.

"Yeah, my knees definitely feel the impact," Jack agreed.

"Have you tried yoga?" Liesel asked.

Eddie elbowed Julianna in the side. "Can you see Jack chanting and doing downward dog?"

Will you tell the captain that he's messing up Jack's game?

Game? What do you mean?

Oh my. You're thick.

I guess so.

"Teach, Pip says to shut up," Julianna said from the corner of her mouth.

Jack and Liesel were now engaged in a deep conversation about the benefits of yoga, not paying them the least bit of attention.

"Tell him that I said 'why don't you make me'," Eddie quipped.

If you do get control over Eddie's body, then that has to be an option. You have to be able to make him shut up on my command.

You mean *when*.

"One of the reasons you might be experiencing muscle spasms is diet," Liesel was now saying to Jack. "Do you eat meat?"

"It starts with some casual conversation about running, and in no time, our chief engineer is going to have Jack dancing around with a rain stick," Eddie joked loud enough for everyone to hear.

Jack cut his eyes at Eddie before saying, "Don't you two have somewhere to be?"

Eddie yawned loudly. "Not immediately. Ricky Bobby is still en route to Paladin system."

Tell the captain he's an idiot, Pip chimed in.

I tell him that all the time. It doesn't affect him.

Grab him by the arm and drag him out of the office, then. He's messing up Jack's chances.

For what?

Lordy, lordy, lord. You two are meant for each other.

What? No!

You and Teach are both as dense as a jar of mayonnaise.

Hey, don't you lump me into the same category with the captain.

You've been lumped.

Julianna grabbed Eddie by the arm and yanked him out to the hallway. "Come on, mayonnaise. Let's go speak with Knox."

"Mayonnaise?" Eddie laughed, allowing himself to the be pulled. "Who you calling salad dressing?"

"It was from Pip," Julianna explained.

"Tell him that he's a monkey's ass."

Tell the captain, 'Okay, see you next Tuesday'.

That doesn't even make any sense.

Sure it does.

"Why the look of confusion?" Eddie asked, giving Julianna a quizzical look.

"Pip said he'll see you next Tuesday? Do you know what that's about?"

An abrupt laugh fell out of Eddie's mouth. "Damn. I see how he plays."

"What?" Julianna asked.

"His name-calling gets mean fast," Eddie said.

Julianna was immediately confused. "Name-calling? How is something to do with Tuesday name-calling?"

"Take the first letter of 'see you next Tuesday'. It's a clever way to call someone a bad name."

Julianna grimaced. "That's not how you spell that word. It starts with a 'C'."

"When did you become an English teacher?" Eddie joked.

"I'm not, I'm just saying," Julianna said.

"Well, you've got to hang with me if you want to know the hip lingo," Eddie said with a wink.

"Not that I would, but why wouldn't you just call someone that word, rather than saying, 'see you next Tuesday'?" Julianna asked.

Eddie shook his head. "Because calling people names is rude, Jules. This is much classier and less insulting."

"Now I'm taking lessons from you on how to be less offensive. Fuck my life," Julianna said with a sigh.

10

Onyx Mental Facility, Onyx Station, Paladin System

Julianna has to be the woman of a thousand disguises, Eddie thought, strolling beside her through the solid white hallways. Her facial expressions, for one, always seemed to be hiding something.

The pantsuit she was currently wearing made her look like a completely different woman. Maybe he'd gotten too used to seeing her in combat clothes and sporting boots to appreciate her more feminine side. It's not that he didn't notice that she was a woman; it was fucking hard to miss. But Julianna was a *different* kind of woman than most.

"You're staring," she said through tight lips.

Eddie shot his focus forward. "Blue is a nice color on you. That's all."

Julianna peered down at the powder blue suit she was wearing. "It's the color of the sky. Everyone looks good in blue."

"I've been on some planets that didn't have a blue sky,"

Eddie imparted, fidgeting with the belt on his slacks. "Tell me again, why did we have to wear starched suits, but Knox here gets to sport his frayed jeans."

"Do you own a pair of frayed jeans?" Julianna asked.

"No." Eddie looked back at Knox, who was trudging along behind them, no enthusiasm in his eyes. "Can I borrow a pair, Knox?"

The kid smiled weakly but didn't answer.

"We need to blend in," Julianna told Eddie. "Believe me, I'd rather not be wearing these shoes—they pinch the fuck out of my toes. But if I strode in here with a holster and my usual bad-ass attitude, then we'd raise suspicion."

"Yeah, I hear you on the shoes," Eddie said, staring down at the loafers he'd been forced to squeeze his giant feet into.

Julianna plastered a polite smile on her face as they neared the nurse's station. The nurses, all dressed in starched scrubs, sat behind the desk with their chins down.

"Hello," Julianna said in a voice that didn't sound at all like her usual one. "We're here to see Bennet Harrison."

Unhurried, the nurse in the middle of the three looked up, running her eyes over Julianna and then Eddie and Knox at her back. "And you are?"

"Samantha Harrison," Julianna stated. "I'm Benny's sister."

The woman, who had grey eyes absent of any joy, darted her gaze at Eddie and Knox. "And they are?"

"Her husband," Eddie said in a rush. It sounded so strange coming out of his mouth, but there it was. "And this is my brother, Chris. Our parents had me first and then Chris here a full decade later. We're best buds now."

"I don't care," the nurse said, her tone dull. She extended a hand to Julianna. "I'm going to need two forms of identification."

Julianna unclipped the purse hanging on her shoulder. Eddie never thought he'd see Julianna carrying a purse unless it had a gun in it; however, this one was full of makeup and other feminine essentials, since she expected to be searched at security.

"Here you are," Julianna said, handing over the fake documents that the general had provided them with. "If you check my brother's file, you'll see that I'm his sister, Samantha Harrison."

The nurse handed back the identification. "I don't care. Second door on the right."

Julianna took the IDs, looking to be holding back a snide remark. "Okay. Thanks. See you next Tuesday."

Julianna knocked on the door to Dr. Bennett Harrison's room.

"I'm naked! Don't come in!" a man yelled in reply.

Julianna turned the handle for the door. Eddie reached out and grabbed her arm, a startled look in his eyes.

"Didn't you hear the man?" Eddie asked. "He's naked."

"It may surprise you, but I've seen my fair share of naked men. Maybe he'll show me something I haven't seen," Julianna stated unabashed.

Eddie glared at her. "Dammit, Fregin. I can't take you anywhere."

"This is how I act out when I'm not allowed to have my gun," Julianna said, turning back to the door.

"Well, as your husband, I insist on going in first," Eddie said, sliding around Julianna to open the door enough to admit him, and then swinging it closed again.

Julianna cast a look back at Knox, who didn't appear at all entertained. "Isn't Mr. Fregin a doll?" she asked him.

"I heard that," Eddie said from the other side of the door. "And it's all clear. Dr. Harrison is completely clothed."

Julianna stepped into the room and immediately ducked.

Bennett sat on a bed in the middle of the room, launching things through the air in her direction. Julianna blocked her head with her arm and looked down at the floor where one of the objects had landed.

"Is that a rubber chicken?" she asked, pointing to the floor.

"Yes," Eddie said, also shielding his head from the strange attack. "But he's only got one more, so we should be okay."

"Which I'm not throwing until you lower your hands," Bennett said in a hoarse voice.

"They're rubber chickens. Not bullets." Julianna rolled her eyes at her partner. "Dr. Harrison, we're here because we really need your help," she said, pulling her arm away from her face.

"Well, our friend Knox does," Eddie said.

A rubber chicken careened into his head.

In an effort to keep a straight face, Eddie brushed his hands down the front of his pin-striped suit.

He looks good, polished. Almost refined, Julianna thought.

I heard that!

Shut the fuck up, Pip.

When I'm in the captain's head, I'll be sure to relay these sweet nothings.

Not if I erase you beforehand.

Your idle threats mean nothing to me.

Would you go away? I'm trying to get a mad man to help us.

Okay. See you next Tuesday.

"Dr. Harrison," Julianna began. "We understand that you're the very best with hypnosis, and we'd—"

"Cluck! Cluck!" The doctor sprang off the bed, flapping his arms by his sides. He hurried over to the fallen rubber chickens laying by their feet. "My babies! Don't step on my babies!" Dr. Harrison gathered up the rubber chickens and piled them on his bed.

Eddie gave Julianna a look that seemed to say, *"This guy is as nutty as a fruitcake,"* However, Julianna wasn't entirely convinced of that. Pip and she had their own speculation about this doctor and now that she was here, she thought they were right. Julianna had met a lot of insane people. Hell, many of them, she'd *made* that way. And this guy... well, he was entertaining, but there was something about the look in his blue eyes that made him seem more lucid than he was playing at. He had stringy gray hair and a face full of wrinkles, but somehow, he still seemed young. Maybe that was because he was petting a rubber chicken.

"I know, Clare," Dr. Harrison said to one of the chickens he was holding. "I'm working on your pen now. Give me another day, and you'll have a proper place to lay your eggs."

"Dr. Harrison, do you still practice any of your old hypnosis strategies?" Julianna pressed.

The man held the chicken up to his ear, like it was a telephone. "Aunt Daisy, I've had the best day at the farm. Let me tell you all about it."

"Jules," Eddie said, his voice a hush. "I don't know if this is going to work. This guy is—"

"Acting," she said firmly, cutting him off.

"What?" Eddie asked, his brow wrinkling.

Dr. Harrison spun around, the chicken still clutched to his ear. "Aunt Daisy, I have to go."

"Doctor, I read your file," Julianna began, "It is very curious indeed. I had my AI cross-reference your symptoms with those of a dozen other patients displaying the same ones. Do you know what we found?"

"That those poor souls died a miserable and lonely death?" Dr. Harrison asked, suddenly scratching his flaky skin. "I'm certain my shingles are back. And my restless leg syndrome is worse than ever; it's going to be a long night for sure."

Julianna ignored his complaints. "Pip and I discovered that those patients were all faking. What I can't figure out, though," she continued, "is why someone with your education in mental illness would do the same."

Eddie spun around to face her, a look of shock on his

face. "He's faking? Are you sure? When were you going to tell me that?" He sounded offended.

"Now," she told him simply.

Dr. Harrison looked to the right and then to the left, as if trying to find a way out of the conversation.

"Doctor, we're not here to hurt you," Julianna stated. "We need your help. If you can give us that, then maybe we can do the same for you. That's got to be better than pretending to be crazy for the rest of your life."

Dr. Harrison slid the rubber chickens off his bed and took a seat, looking defeated. "Pretending to be crazy is better than lying in a casket."

"So you are faking it," Eddie declared triumphantly.

The man nodded.

"Why, though?" Julianna asked. "And why are you, an expert in mental illness, displaying every symptom imaginable?"

"The treatment of mental illness has progressed rapidly under the Federation," Dr. Harrison explained. "We can stabilize even the most serious cases of mental illness, which means most patients are released from this institute within three years."

"But you can't be released if you have an illness that's not classified," Julianna stated, figuring it out at once.

"Now the question remains, why are you faking being crazy?" Eddie asked.

"How easy was it for you to get in here?" Dr. Harrison asked.

"Well, for a normal person, it would have taken a formal written request, a submission of identification records to the board, and a background check, along with a pat-down upon entry," Julianna stated.

"I'm guessing you're not normal people," Dr. Harrison said with a morbid laugh.

"We work for a powerful man," Julianna said. "You also have probably guessed that we're not the bad guys who are trailing you."

"No because they have fish breath and a dorsal fin," Dr. Harrison explained.

"So the Trid are after you," Eddie summated.

Dr. Harrison nodded. "You must have connections to get in here so easily. For most it takes a clearance and cutting through a lot of red tape."

"You've been faking being crazy to remain protected inside this facility?" he asked. "What kind of life is that?"

"It's an easy one," Dr. Harrison admitted. "I've worked my entire life, tirelessly producing research for journals and doing everything I can to make myself an asset to the mental health community. Now I wake up, do what I like and eat pudding for breakfast. It's really the life I've been pining for."

"Then your secret is safe with us," Julianna stated. "But in return, we'd like you to take one last patient."

She stepped to the side and presented Knox, who had been standing in the corner like a shadow.

The bed smells like the old man, Knox noted as he nestled deeper into the sheets.

"That's it," Dr. Harrison encouraged. "Make yourself comfortable. The more relaxed you are, the better."

Right, Knox thought. *Just lay down in a stranger's bed and relax. No big deal.*

"With your eyes closed, I want you to continue to focus on my voice," Dr. Harrison said. "It will be your guide. Wherever it tells you to go, you go. My voice is your ruler, and you must do whatever it says."

Dude. This guy has some gnarly skills, if he can really control people with his voice. No wonder he's hiding from the Trid.

"Now, even though you are incredibly relaxed, you're not going to sleep," Dr. Harrison ordered.

"I'm not going to sleep," Knox said, and was surprised to hear his own voice. *Whoa. I didn't even think that...*

The old man had already taken Knox through three guided meditations, mostly involving sitting calmly in the forest or lying on a beach. There was a freedom in Knox's mind that he'd never known before.

"Let's begin with what you did today, from the moment you woke up," Dr. Harrison prompted.

Knox's eyes moved under his closed lids.

"Do you recall that clearly?" Dr. Harrison asked.

"Yes," the boy answered.

Dr. Harrison had agreed to help Knox and keep his findings confidential in exchange for Ghost Squadron's promise to keep the doctor's sanity a secret. Julianna and Eddie had readily agreed, and briefed the doctor on what they needed Knox to remember. They'd also given Dr.

Harrison certain details about Knox's life that would help trigger the memory.

"Good, good. Now, what about the day you were reunited with your father? Can you recall that day in its entirety?"

"Yes, I remember that day," Knox stated.

"That's fantastic," Dr. Harrison said. "I want you to go back further. Can you remember the day your father took you to the aquarium?"

Knox had been seven years old, and it was one of his favorite memories. He thought of it often, so he had no trouble calling it up now.

"Yes, I can," he answered.

"Wonderful," Dr. Harrison cheered. "Now, can you recall the day that your father disappeared?"

Knox's head tightened. His eyes flinched. His fingers clenched.

"Take a deep breath, my boy. It's only a memory," Dr. Harrison said.

Knox saw a swirling of colors: reds, blues, browns, greens. They all spiraled together until turning crisp and forming the picture of Knox's childhood home. He was walking through it, calling out for his father. It was like the vision he'd seen in his old house, when he'd tried to recall the memory the first time.

"I see it," Knox said, his voice a whisper.

"That's great," Dr. Harrison declared. "That memory is easy to recall. You can see as much of it as you want. You can zoom in on specific details, and even rewind it if you like. Did you know that?"

Knox felt his head shake. "I didn't."

"It's true. That one memory is clearer than any other, and the more you study it, the more you remember. Isn't that wonderful?"

Knox felt his mouth smile. "Yes."

"Now, tell me what you see as you play the memory," Dr. Harrison said, his tone neutral.

"I'm walking through my house, looking for my father," Knox began.

"Do you find him?" Dr. Harrison asked.

Knox shook his head against the pillow. "No, I go out to his workshop. I see the Tangle Thief."

"That's nice. What do you do next?"

"I reach out and take it. I think it will take me to my father," Knox said, living it like it was his present reality. He felt the object in his hand as his fingers wrapped around it. He sucked in a breath and initiated the device. It was all coming back to him; this was where the memory had stopped before.

"Where does the Tangle Thief take you?" Dr. Harrison asked.

Knox saw only blackness. He was certain the memory had vanished, like before. He let out a breath, about to sit up and admit defeat, when he was suddenly able to make out high walls and hundreds of storage units filling the space around him. The locker in front of him popped open when his feet hit the ground, after being transported. Inside the drawer was another Tangle Thief, both the receptor and client pieces.

"Area 126," Knox stated quietly.

"Lovely. A fine place, I'm sure," the doctor said.

"There's a woman…I think it's a woman," Knox said, speeding through the vision. Dr. Harrison was right; he could see to the end of the memory, and then rewind it. He could slow it down and hone in on details.

"A woman of sorts. Very nice. What happens next?" Dr. Harrison asked.

Knox bolted upright in the bed, suddenly breathless. He'd fast forwarded until he'd seen where the hologram had sent him.

Eddie and Julianna were both staring at him with wide eyes.

"You're not supposed to come out until I say," the doctor admonished.

Knox was trying to pull oxygen into his lungs. "I saw where Kyra sent me. I was placed under the protection of Alleira. In Sunex."

After a moment of shocked silence, Julianna turned to Eddie. "Where you were nearly blown to bits…" Her voice was haunted.

11

Fat Cat's Karaoke Bar, Onyx Station, Paladin System

Visiting hours had ended shortly after Knox's revelation. With a reminder from Dr. Harrison of the promise they'd made, the members of Ghost Squadron left the good doctor to himself.

Eddie was happy they had a lead, and that they were familiar with Alleira and her people. They'd helped to protect them from the Brotherhood, so Eddie was certain that they'd be happy to return the favor and tell them what happened to Knox while he was with them.

"You don't remember anything after being transported to Sunex?" Julianna asked Knox for the tenth time.

He shook his head. His mohawk had gone limp and now lay on one side of his head, seemingly exhausted, just like Knox.

Undergoing hypnosis must be taxing, Julianna mused.

"I remember landing and meeting Alleira. That's it," he admitted.

"How were you even able to resist the hypnosis and come out early?" Julianna asked.

"Like Dr. Harrison said, it's all suggestive," Knox said, stirring his drink. He hadn't taken a sip yet, and most of the ice had melted.

"We've got a place to look next, and that's better than what we had before our little visit," Eddie said, taking a sip of his beer.

"And we have shots," Lars chimed in, setting four shot glasses down on the table and nearly spilling them.

"Shots?" Julianna asked, looking between the overfilled glasses and then to Lars. "When did you become the alcoholic of the group?"

"He made me get them," Lars said, pointing at Eddie.

"Guilty as charged," Eddie said, waving Chester and Marilla forward. They were carrying their own shots from the bar, eyeing the drinks like they were lava.

"You won't be happy until you have the whole crew sloshed, will you?" Julianna asked him.

"I think we need a little time off, is all," Eddie said, lifting his shot glass in the air. "Cheers to being a part of a great team, who I'd fight a pack of giraffe assassins to protect."

Julianna lifted her glass and paused. "*Giraffe* assassins?"

"With telescoping legs and necks," Chester sang, clinking his glass with the others.

"Cheers," everyone said in unison, before tossing back their heads and downing their drinks.

"Wow, that burns," Marilla choked out, gripping her throat.

"Does it?" Julianna asked, placing her shot glass in the row with her other empties.

Eddie threw his thumb in her direction. "This woman has hair on her chest. Don't listen to her."

Julianna had abandoned her blazer and unbuttoned her blouse a couple notches. "I find it a little insulting that, since I can handle my liquor, I'm being compared to a man."

Marilla nodded defiantly. "I agree. I think we should turn those references around on these guys."

"Come on, ladies," Eddie urged. "It's not like that."

"No, no," Julianna argued. "When someone is a coward, what do you usually say?"

Eddie looked to Lars for support, but the lieutenant had found his drink and was using it as a distraction. "I-I-I usually say they should grow a pair."

"Exactly!" Julianna said, taking a drink. "Do you mean a pair of boobs?"

"I mean—"

"And the other day, what did you call that pirate who'd looted a bunch of ships?" Julianna asked, leaning back and looking interested in the answer.

"The one I threw off the upper deck of the ship he'd stolen?" Eddie asked, needing to clarify. There had been so many pirates that it was easy to get confused.

"That's the one," Julianna sang.

"I think I called him a pussy," Eddie said meekly.

"Oh, right," Julianna took the shot that Chester handed to her.

The hacker also pushed one in Marilla's direction. He

was staying quiet during this witch hunt; Eddie wished he could do the same, but he'd already been tied to the stake.

"Hey, I call jerks 'dicks,'" Eddie argued. "I'm not sexist."

"Jerks are dicks," Julianna stated.

Eddie lifted his beer, trying to catch Julianna's eye, but she had her gaze stubbornly on the table. *Is she actually mad about this? Or about something else?* He wished he could ask Pip.

"I sincerely apologize if I offended you ladies," he said. "I'll quit calling dumb fuckers by gender-specific names, and comparing you to a man when you do something totally badass. I hope you know I'm capable of change."

Everyone at the table fell silent, and their gazes fell on Julianna, like they were waiting for her lead.

She finally lifted her eyes, a sort-of-smile on her face. "I think, Captain, that you can be a real dick." She paused before lifting her glass. "But for that matter, so can I. All is forgiven when you can admit your mistakes."

———

It's a little hypocritical, that's all I'm saying.

Julianna ground her teeth together. Pip was right, but admitting it was difficult.

You're guilty of gender-specific name-calling, too. It's not just the captain.

Yeah, whatever. The captain had it coming.

Did he?

He did.

Because...

He breathes too loudly while I'm flying.

Pip made an audible gasp. **Say it isn't so? Blasphemy.**

It's annoying.

Does he also snore while sleeping?

How would I know?

I'll tell you when I'm linked with him. I'll tell you all sorts of things.

Julianna tried her best to ignore Pip, pretending to pay attention to the karaoke singer who was making a debauchery of "Thunderstruck" by AC/DC.

From the look on Eddie's face, he was just as unhappy about the travesty.

"Is nothing sacred anymore?" he asked her, running his finger over the rim of his glass.

"We're in a karaoke bar. What do you expect?" she asked, pushing her empty glass in his direction.

"Is that your subtle way of asking for me to get you another drink?" Eddie asked, his face full of amusement.

"That's my subtle way of saying 'if I'm not supplied with more whiskey, then the guy onstage is going to lose a limb,'" Julianna said.

Eddie stood and bowed slightly. "Then I'm honored to be a part of this public service."

Julianna didn't remember when she'd last drank this much. It wasn't that she was drunk, but she was buzzed, which was rare. She strangely felt like saying something supportive to Knox, who was still sulking. Or maybe she'd say something nice to Lars, who actually looked to be having a good time as he tapped his foot to the horrible music.

They must not have good music on Kezza, she thought.

Then she turned to Marilla. The girl looked—well, there was no better way to say it. She looked miserable. Maybe it was being on Onyx Station, which was vibrating with life and diverse experiences.

Is ship life starting to get to Marilla? She is used to sunshine and trekking through the forest on archeological digs...

"Hey, Marilla?" Julianna said, getting her attention.

The woman looked up, faking a smile. "Yes?"

"Do you want to go with us to Nexus? The land of Sunex is considered safe; maybe you can offer some insight when we're dealing with the natives," Julianna said.

Marilla nodded, her mood seeming to brighten. "That would be lovely. Thanks."

"Then it's settled," Julianna said.

She noticed that Knox perked up at the mention of Sunex. She imagined he was probably both longing to track down the Tangle Thief and dreading it. There was a lot riding on his shoulders, and anything she might say in an attempt to comfort him would be a lie, so she decided not to say anything.

"Okay, thanks to Greg for the fantastic rendition of 'Thunderstruck'," the karaoke DJ said over the microphone.

"'Fantastic'?" Eddie said in disbelief, sliding a drink next to Julianna as he took a seat.

"The guy is obviously deaf," Julianna said, nodding her thanks in the direction of the shot of whiskey.

"Up next, we have a classic Beatles song," the DJ said,

squinting down at the screen in front of him. "Please welcome to the stage, Chester!"

Everyone at the table whipped around to find *their* Chester jumping onto the stage, holding up his hands to excited applause.

"Yeah, baby!" Chester yelled, eating up the attention.

Eddie leaned over and said, "When do you think that poor guy is going to come out of his shell?"

Julianna took a sip of her whiskey. "All we can do is keep coercing him."

"Thank you! Thank you!" Chester boomed, taking the microphone. "I want to dedicate this song to someone."

Julianna and Eddie looked at each other, the same hesitation in their eyes.

"You see, there's this girl," Chester continued. "And she's mad at me because I won't say what she deserves to hear."

The crowd let out a chorus of "awes" and "ohs."

Chester nodded, shrugging. He had both hands locked around the microphone, and his gaze was aimed down at the floor. "It's true, but sometimes we don't want to tell someone how we feel because we fear their rejection."

"Yay!" the crowd cheered.

"This is either going to go over great, or we're going to have issues," Eddie whispered in Julianna's ear.

"But I think when two people feel something, and neither is willing to admit it...well, there's stress," Chester said, now sounding like he was lecturing.

"It hurts so good!" someone in the crowd yelled.

Chester pointed at his new fan. "Exactly, brother.

Anyway, this song is my way of telling someone special that she's, well, special."

Chester lifted the microphone and looked directly at their table.

The piano began. Chester cleared his throat. "Hey, Marilla," he sang, changing the words for "Hey Jude."

To no one's surprise, Marilla covered her reddened face with her hands. Julianna probably would have clocked Chester for such a thing, but she suspected that Marilla liked it. And now she recognized why the comms officer had appeared so melancholy lately.

Love makes you crazy.

How would you know?

I've been in love before.

With who?

It's better if I confess this in a song.

Ugh. Don't.

Pip coughed, like clearing his throat. He started to sing, doing the worst impression ever of Aerosmith's *I Don't Want to Miss a Thing*.

I'm about to throw up.

Pip continued to sing.

Julianna downed the rest of her whiskey, which earned her a curious look from Eddie. He'd been watching Chester's impressive rendition of the Beatles classic.

"What's Pip saying?" he asked.

"He's trying to murder my soul," Julianna explained.

Eddie shoved his unfinished drink in Julianna's direction. "Then you need this more than I do."

The crowd had now fully joined in with Chester, clapping in the air over their heads.

Chester sang, his hand directed at Marilla who now had her fingers pressed to her chest and an elated smile on her face.

"They are going to be unbearable now," Julianna said in a hush.

Eddie leaned back, a thoughtful expression in his eyes. "I think they'll be better all around. Love makes us stronger."

Julianna studied Eddie. "I never took you for a romantic."

He tilted his head to the side. "I'm absolutely not. But I've seen enough to know what a good relationship can do for someone. My parents, for instance."

And there they were; the demons returned in a flash, dancing behind Eddie's eyes. They would surface at the mere mention of his parents. This time, though, the expression on his face was a mix of pain and fondness—like thinking of them simultaneously haunted him and brought him comfort.

"Sounds like they had a good thing," Julianna ventured.

"They did," Eddie said simply. "Something rare that you hardly ever see."

She didn't know what else to say, but thankfully the crowd erupted, joining in with Chester for the end of the song.

"Hey Marilla."

Chester busted out the last note, sliding down to his knees and singing passionately for all the bar to see.

Marilla bolted out of her seat, leaping around crowded tables on her way to the stage.

Julianna turned her attention fully to Eddie, who also didn't look keen on watching the display of affection that was about to ensue. "So, you and Chester think you can pull off a rendition of 'Bohemian Rhapsody'?"

"Yes and fuck yes!" Eddie said, smiling wide.

12

Alpha-line Q-Ship, Nexus, Tangki System

Fletcher scratched his chin and turned his attention to Lars. The pilot was strictly focused on staying in formation behind the captain and the commander's ship.

"Nexus is a beautiful planet," Fletcher said, hoping his voice sounded natural.

"Incredibly so," Lars agreed.

"The area we explored last time was to the east." Fletcher pointed in the direction of Area 126.

"Yes. I heard that the facility you searched had many oddities," Lars said, making their descent to the lush land below.

Fletcher laughed. " 'Odd' is the right word for it. There was a family tree that I found. It...well, never mind. You're probably not interested."

Lars darted his beady, lizard-like eyes at Fletcher, interest obviously written in them. "It what?"

Fletcher hoped he was playing this right. As the new

XO for the ship, he had access to all the crew's files, and therefore knew that Lars had lost both his parents at a young age. "Well, this family tree allows the person in front of it to talk to any of their ancestors who have passed over."

"No way," Lars stated.

"It's true," Fletcher said. "I talked to my grandmother."

"How do you know it was her?" Lars asked.

Fletcher laughed easily. "Only one woman could taunt me the way that old lady did."

Lars looked halfway between wanting to believe and not thinking he should. "No. There's really such an object?"

"I swear it," Fletcher promised.

"Man, it would be amazing to have five minutes with this family tree." Lars lowered the Q-Ship, landing it smoothly.

"I still have the access badge to get into the facility," Fletcher said matter-of-factly. He knew that, as XO, he could order Lars to take him, but motivation was key here.

"Yeah, but how are we going to get away? We have a mission," Lars said, sounding defeated.

"True," Fletcher agreed. "But we do have to sleep at some point. Unless you think you can give up a few hours of shut-eye for a rogue mission…"

"I do sleep less than most," Lars admitted.

"Then it's settled," Fletcher said at once. "You fly, and I'll get us into Area 126."

"But what about the captain and commander?" Lars asked.

"What about them?"

"Do you think they'll mind?"

Fletcher shrugged. "I don't see why they would. It's not like we're doing anything to undermine the current mission. What we do on our own time is our business."

"Yeah, I guess you're right," Lars allowed.

Fletcher celebrated a silent victory. He'd secured what he needed for the next phase of his plan: a pilot to get him to the island where Area 126 was located.

If he was honest with himself, the whole endeavor was reckless. He knew that diverting his attention from the current mission was a risk. But how could he not take this opportunity to try and speak to his father? He'd had that chance stolen the last time he was in Area 126. It was time he had closure. It was time he got to say goodbye.

Nona leaned forward from the second row of the Q-Ship's seats. Lately she'd spotted the restlessness in Fletcher's eyes. She'd asked her lieutenant many times if something was bothering him; a question most couldn't get away with. However, Fletcher didn't seem to mind her questions. But he never answered them honestly.

The team's spirited chatter made it hard for Nona to discern Fletcher and Lars's conversation in the front of the Q-Ship. She was sure she'd heard them mention 'family tree'.

She leaned in further, about to fall out of her seat.

If I can just get a little closer... Nona picked up her canteen, wedged it into her pack, and pretended to take a sip. When she screwed the lid back into place, she dropped the container, allowing it to roll to the front of the ship.

"Oops," she said, but no one was paying her any attention, anyway.

Nona hurried after the water canteen, grabbing it when she was just behind the lieutenant's seat. She stayed down low, listening intently to the conversation between Fletcher and the pilot. She navigated back to her seat just as the ship landed.

"What's that, to the west?" Julianna asked over the comm.

Eddie squinted over the rolling green hills, the setting sun partially obscuring his vision. On the plains that bordered the forests, dust clouds hung over a great commotion.

"I'm going back up for a closer look," Eddie stated, pulling back on the controls, lifting the Q-Ship into the air.

He cloaked the ship—something they hadn't done when arriving on Sunex. He'd figured that since it was considered the safest place on Nexus back when Knox had been transported there, cloaking wouldn't be necessary. Maybe it had been a mistake to think that the land would still be safe.

Eddie zoomed the Q-Ship closer to the action, and immediately saw what was responsible for the disturbance. Sunex might have been considered a place of peace a decade ago, but something was seeking to destroy that now.

"The Petigren are attacking the natives," Eddie said over the comm.

Julianna shot a sideways look at Knox in the copilot seat. His face automatically turned a shade of green.

"Looks like the Saverus are one step ahead of us," Julianna stated, cloaking her ship.

"Fucking slippery snakes," Eddie said with a sigh. "However, they haven't breached the camp's borders yet."

Julianna released the hatch door of her Q-Ship, turning to face the Special Forces unit seated in the rear. "Take out all Petigren. Be cautious, though; the Saverus could be out there, looking like anyone."

The soldiers saluted before filing out the back.

"Carnivore, what's your status?" Julianna asked Lars over the comm.

"Ground forces have been dispersed," he reported.

"Good," Julianna said. "I want you to fly overhead and provide cover. Focus on keeping these rat-fuckers away from the perimeter of the camp."

"Copy that, Strong Arm," Lars confirmed.

"Black Beard," Julianna said. "I'm taking Mohawk to the village center."

"I'll meet you there," Eddie said.

Fletcher sent teams one and two to take the battle to the

perimeter. "Team three, hit them straight on," he said, throwing two fingers at the fight.

The soldiers took off at a sprint, weapons in hand. Once on the ground, Fletcher could tell that the natives were losing the fight. He wasn't surprised. Inhabitants of Sunex were not equipped for war, which is why Ghost Squadron had already saved them from the Brotherhood once.

These people can't catch a break, Fletcher thought, taking off.

The Petigren, as he knew from experience, didn't fight fair. He watched as two rat-men attacked one of the natives from behind, one taking out his legs, and the other sinking his sharp teeth into the back of the man's neck.

Fletcher picked up speed, launching his foot forward when he was only a couple feet away. The Petigren looked up in time to see the bottom of Fletcher's boot connect with his hairy face. Pulling the butt of his rifle around, Fletcher clubbed the second Petigren over the head.

A rat-like man whipped around from the kill it'd just made, blood dripping down from his chin. A cackle spilled out of its mouth before it launched in Fletcher's direction. The Petigren didn't make it another step before a bullet struck it down.

Fletcher dared to turn around, and found Nona standing a few yards behind him, her rifle at the ready. "Thanks," he told her.

Her eyes darted to something at his back. With reflexes to impress, she moved the rifle an inch and fired. Another approaching Petigren fell.

Fletcher slung his rifle over his back and pulled the knife from his boot. He lunged into the thick of the fighting, where the natives were using their fists to fight the Petigren. Nona could take the perimeter, but someone needed to make a dent in the major artery of the fight before things spun out of control.

Fletcher stabbed a Petigren in the back, keeping him from choking one of the long-haired natives. The beast fell. With a quick breath, Fletcher wrapped his arm around the neck of another Petigren, slicing its throat in a single movement. Bodies were crammed tightly together in this pocket of the battle, which meant that Fletcher had to act fast before the natives were overwhelmed.

Dovon elbowed the face of the rat-creature closest to him. The animal dropped.

Dovon's people, the Sunexans, might not know how to fight, but they were larger than the aliens and much stronger. He pulled an axe from his belt and launched it through the air, taking down another monster bounding for him.

Around him, he could see his people were losing. They didn't have the prowess to overtake these enemies; fighting wasn't in their blood. And there were too many of the creatures.

The lookout had spotted at least a hundred of the giant rats. Alleira had ordered the strongest to cut the enemy off before they got to the border. They'd already been pushed back so far, though.

Dovon whipped a large stick around, slamming it into a Petigren's face. The beast wasn't as easily deterred as the others had been, and kept after him, knocking Dovon to the ground. Dovon kicked at the rat, but it chomped at his legs, from its position on all fours. Scrambling back, Dovon took up a rock. He threw it hard, slamming it into the monster's face. The Petigren rolled to the side.

Dovon glanced at his back as he scrambled to a standing position. The gates to the Sunexans' land was only a few yards away.

He feared they'd lost this battle. Disappointed Alleira.

Another Petigren charged for him, this one looking more rabid than the others. Dovon frantically searched; he was out of weapons. The monster would be on him in seconds. He was about to turn and run for the border, when a man with a bald head and dressed in a black uniform shot seemingly out of nowhere. He grabbed the rat around the neck, halting him immediately. With his other hand, he stabbed a knife through the enemy's chest. The Petigren shrieked loudly in its death throes.

The man dropped the giant rat and spun around, as if aware of the attack approaching from behind. Two more of the horrible creatures had snuck up on him. The man reached forward, grabbing one by the hand, and yanking it over his head as he spun around. He flung it to the ground like it weighed nothing at all. The other rat jumped onto the man's back, but he wasn't startled. Instead, he yanked his arm holding his knife up over his head, and stabbed the creature straight in the back.

Shrugging off the dead beasts, the man spun to face Dovon. "Get inside your borders. This is our fight; no more from Sunex shall be harmed."

Dovon nodded, in a daze from the battle, before turning and sprinting for the fence.

Julianna landed her Q-Ship beside Eddie's. Those from Sunex were already gathered around the main communal area, their tanned faces looking apprehensively at the ship.

The air was crisp and laced with an ocean breeze as Julianna stepped out of the Q-Ship. She hoped that the Sunexans would recognize her and be put at ease.

Lars has been successful at pushing the Petigren back from the perimeter, Pip reported.

Good. What about the ground forces? Julianna asked.

They are taking a beating, but thinning the numbers dramatically.

And the Sunexans?

They are being sent back into the protected territory.

Good. I'll relay that information to Alleira.

Tell her I think she's pretty.

You never tell me you think I'm pretty.

No, no I don't.

The leader of Sunex stood in front of her people, her long, almost white blonde hair, braided into four different sections. Her white robes contrasted with her tanned skin and made her bright blue eyes pop. She was no doubt beautiful, as were all from Sunex.

Julianna turned back to find Knox still hanging by the Q-Ship. He blinked around at the people, staring like he was trying to recognize them.

Julianna waved him forward. "Come on. We're going to get answers."

Eddie hurried over, Marilla and Chester behind him.

Alleira's eyes darted to the warfare at Julianna's back as she stepped forward. Many of the Sunexans' faces contorted with pain as the sounds of slaughter traveled across the hills.

"Ghost Squadron, do you know about these attacks?" Alleira asked.

"Yes, and we know who is behind them," Julianna stated. "We will have them under control soon. Your people are being sent back inside the security of the border."

"Good. We thank you," Alleira said, her eyes darting to Knox by Julianna's side.

"We need to speak with you immediately," Eddie interjected, his tone urgent.

"Of course." Alleira held up her hand, motioning to a large tent in the distance. "Follow me to my quarters."

Julianna nodded and joined the leader of the peaceful people. The people parted, many of the children looking at the strangers with amused expressions.

"The Petigren, the ones attacking you, when did this start?" Julianna asked.

"We spotted them an hour ago," Alleira answered. "Your timing was a blessing."

"I think it was luck," Julianna said.

"You sent men out to defend the land from the Petigren, correct?" Eddie asked.

"I sent my people out to see what these creatures you call the Petigren wanted," Alleira explained. "Defense isn't our first mode of thinking. We don't just expect warfare; we're quite surprised that's the option others choose."

"Have any of those men from the first group returned?" Eddie asked.

Julianna knew what Eddie was getting at. If the Petigren were here, then the Saverus weren't far away. It was entirely possible that they were impersonating one of the Sunexans.

Alleira shook her head. "They were attacked immediately. After that, I sent another group to defend our borders."

Eddie gave Julianna a cautious look. "To be safe, we request an audience with only you, Alleira. We must be very careful."

Alleira spun around at the entrance to her tent. Hers was larger than the others and covered in a green netting that made it blend in with its surroundings. The leader of the Sunexans darted her eyes to the man by her side, who was shirtless and wore feathers in his long hair. "You will leave us here."

"But my queen—" the man argued.

"I'm quite safe with Ghost Squadron," Alleira cut him off.

"As you wish. I'm here if you need anything." He nodded, pulling back the tent flap for them to enter.

———

Eddie threw off his jacket upon entering Alleira's quarters. The tent smelled of burning herbs and was stiflingly hot. Marilla and Chester had stayed back, giving Marilla a chance to study the Sunexans. She had never been exposed to their culture.

Chester accompanied her 'out of curiosity', but Eddie sensed it was more because he didn't want to be out of Marilla's presence. *Oh, to be in love and never tire of someone,* he thought fondly.

Alleira's long, white robe billowed when she swept around to face them, her hands pressed together in front of her. "This attack... it is about you, isn't it?" she asked, her gaze on Knox.

He straightened between Eddie and Julianna.

"You recognize our friend, Knox?" Eddie asked.

"Of course," Alleira stated. "Although you've grown since I last saw you."

"How long ago was that?" Julianna questioned.

Alleira blinked, seeming to muse on the question. "It would be close to ten years, now. He called himself 'Dominic' then."

"The Petigren and Saverus are attacking Sunex because they want to know what happened to Knox," Eddie explained. "More specifically, they want to know what he did with a device after coming to your land."

"Will you please tell us about Knox's time here?" Julianna asked.

Alleira gave him a curious look. "Do you not remember, Dominic?"

Knox shook his head, his hands pressed firmly into his pockets and his shoulders pinned up high.

Alleira sighed. "You were young and, I suspect, had undergone a major tragedy. I'm grateful to see you, as I have worried for quite some time that something bad happened to you."

"What?" Eddie asked. "Can you start from the beginning?"

Alleira nodded. "One day, Dominic appeared in the center of the village. He said that a woman named Kyra had sent him to us to keep him safe. Since he was a child and no obvious threat to us, we vowed to do just that. However, the night that Knox appeared, I had a dream. My people have long trusted our dreams to give us insight and direction. This dream told me that although Dominic would be safe within our borders, he would never feel accepted. Differences in appearance, unfortunately, divide even peaceful civilizations."

Eddie studied Knox. With his black hair and pale skin, he would certainly stick out among those from Sunex.

"I made arrangements to send the boy to Federation Border Station 7," Alleira continued. "I set it up so that he would be welcomed by a loving family, and offered everything he would need to flourish."

Julianna shot a curious look at Knox. "Are you remembering any of this?"

He shook his head.

"Dominic never arrived on Border Station 7," Alleira said. "I later received word that the ship he'd been on experienced an engine failure, and crashed on an unidentified planet, with no survivors."

"That's how you ended up on Planet L2SCQ-6," Eddie inferred, grateful to finally be getting more puzzle pieces.

"Your report must have been wrong," Julianna said, throwing her arm in Knox's direction. "He obviously survived."

"I see that it must have been," Alleira stated. "I'm grateful for the error."

"Knox, or rather the boy you knew as 'Dominic', would have had a few pieces of a device with him," Eddie began. "Do you remember that?"

"Yes, of course I do," Alleira said. "They were odd, but nothing of interest to us."

"Are you saying you don't have the device?" Julianna asked.

Alleira shook her head. "It was not ours to keep, nor do we have an interest in anything technological. It is counterintuitive to the peace we work hard to maintain through living simply."

"You sent me, along with the device," Knox said, his voice a ghostly whisper.

"Knox? Are you remembering something?" Eddie asked.

Knox shook his head and then corrected himself by nodding. "I only saw a flash. I was on a ship, and on my lap was a wooden box that contained the Tangle Thief. At least, I think that's what was in there."

"Yes, the box was a gift from us," Alleira said with a smile.

"Well, that doesn't tell us much, but at least we know that the Tangle Thief isn't here," Eddie said with a sigh.

"And we know that it might be on Planet L2SCQ-6," Julianna offered.

"It's an electronic," Chester said, handing his pad to a little girl with cerulean eyes. She blinked back at him.

"Go ahead, take it," he urged. "There are a few games that I think you'll like."

"The people here don't use electronic devices," Marilla said at his side.

"I know." Chester rolled his eyes. "I'm trying to educate them. Just you wait, they're going to thank me."

"What if you destroy their innocence?" Marilla argued.

The little girl had taken the pad. Her eyes widened when Chester swiped his finger across the screen, and it lit up.

"Here, you'll like this game. Just try and match three candies in a row," Chester explained.

"What's candy?" the girl asked.

"And one day you'll be credited with destroying the last remaining peaceful society in the galaxy," Marilla said with a laugh.

Chester gave her a sideways smile. "Hey, this isn't *The Gods Must Be Crazy*."

"Did you just make a movie reference?" Marilla asked.

Chester laughed. "I'm surprised you got it."

"I'm an anthropologist, and that movie is a beautiful example of what can happen to a primitive civilization that encounters technology," Marilla explained.

"So I shouldn't show this little girl how to play online slots?" Chester joked.

Marilla shook her head. "I'm going to take soil samples. Try not to corrupt the natives."

"I make no promises," Chester called as she retreated.

Verdok slipped the braids tied with feathers off his shoulder. He couldn't understand why the primitive people of Sunex weighed themselves down with long hair. He'd shapeshifted into the queen's chief advisor days ago.

Verdok had almost concluded that the task was a waste, having learned nothing about the boy or the location of the Tangle Thief. If he had to sit around a fire and chant useless verses one more time, he was going to explode.

He had been about to abandon the mission when the elders of the council had apparently taken matters into their own hands. They had to have been the ones to send in the siege of Petigren, resorting to force rather than stealth. They were growing impatient, which meant Verdok was going to be under fire. They'd execute him if he didn't produce results soon.

The elders' impulsive move had worked in Verdok's favor. He had been inside the border when the attack happened, so no one suspected him of being a Saverus.

Now Ghost Squadron had done all the work for him, in asking these questions. He pulled away from where he was stationed behind Alleira's tent, having heard enough. *Planet L2SCQ-6.* That's where he'd go next.

The council would have to give him another chance. He had procured this information, whereas all they'd done was sacrifice hundreds of Petigren.

———————

Having spent most of the evening helping to treat the injured from Sunex, Fletcher's team was exhausted. They'd set up a camp outside the border perimeter.

It hadn't taken long for the ground forces to overwhelm the Petigren, and now the dead were piled up and burning in the distance.

Fletcher didn't think it was possible that the Petigren would return, but Eddie and Julianna wanted the team to remain in position, just in case. Things couldn't be set up any better: the captain and commander were inside the border of Sunex, and Fletcher and his team were on the outskirts.

Nodding to a group gathered around a fire, Fletcher ambled toward the closest Q-Ship. Lars was dutifully checking the controls when he entered.

Good, the pilot didn't bail on me, Fletcher thought.

"We'll be ready to go in five minutes," Lars stated when Fletcher took the copilot's seat.

"Sounds good," Fletcher said, his adrenaline starting to beat in his veins.

"Are you sure you can get us into Area 126?" Lars asked.

Fletcher wrapped his hands around his head and leaned back. "Of course."

"What if we're questioned?" Lars asked.

"Why would we be questioned?" Fletcher countered.

"Because what you're doing is wrong and you know it," a voice chimed in behind him.

Both Fletcher and Lars shot around in their seats. Nona stood in the doorway, her hands on her hips and a stubborn look on her face.

"Officer Fuller, what are you doing here?" Fletcher asked, his voice automatically going into lieutenant mode.

"Stopping you from doing something stupid," Nona said, and then cast her gaze at Lars. "Stopping both of you from doing something you'll regret."

Fletcher narrowed his eyes at her. "This is none of your business."

"Oh, really? You're abandoning your post," Nona challenged. "That's not my business?"

She knew she could get away with standing up to him. They both knew it.

"I'm not abandoning my post," Fletcher lied.

"You're not headed to Area 126?" Nona shot back.

Fletcher ran his hands over his shaved head. "Well, yes, we are, but it's to help Ghost Squadron with something."

Nona shook her head, not buying it. "So you're not going to see the family tree located at Area 126?"

How did she know about that? Fletcher ground his teeth together. "We have business there."

"The lieutenant is taking me into Area 126 so that I can speak to my parents," Lars cut in.

Dammit, Kezzin. Fletcher should have guessed that Lars would rat them out at the first chance. *He is honest to a fault.*

"Lars, don't be fooled," Nona said, her gaze on Fletcher. "The lieutenant needs you to take him there because he wants to say goodbye to his father. He's using you."

"Dammit, Fuller, you're out of line," Fletcher was almost yelling.

Nona dared to march forward until she was looking straight up at him. "I don't care. You can't bring him back. I know it sucks. I know it isn't right. My own father committed suicide. How much do you think I want to talk to him, to hear his reasons?"

Fletcher softened. "Nona, this is different."

She shook her head, more adamant than he'd ever seen her. "It's not different! We've all lost someone but none of us are meant to talk to them again. You think you're going to have closure after you hear your father's voice?"

"Yes, I do!" Fletcher yelled.

"All you'll do is tear open a wound that will be even more impossible to heal," Nona reasoned.

"There's a viable way to talk to my father, and you want me to ignore that?" Fletcher's fists were balled by his side.

"Talking to him isn't going to change anything about the past," Nona said, her voice calmer now. "Abandoning your post is only going to make things a hell of a lot worse right now... and you know that, even if you've worked hard to rationalize this."

Lars reached out and pressed his hand down on Fletcher's shoulder. "She's right. We can't bring them back. We can't say anything that they don't already know. They don't need us to say goodbye or tell them that we love them. Being able to let go of our parents is how we know the love was real."

Fletcher pressed his eyelids together. He wanted to argue. More than anything, though, he wanted to punish Nona for interfering.

"What if I helped you with something that is within your control?" Nona asked.

Fletcher opened his eyes, his curiosity taking over.

"You can't bring your father back," she repeated. "But you *can* take out the alien who murdered him."

"Rosco," Fletcher bit on the word.

Nona nodded. "What if, on our time off, I help you track him down? Help you take him out."

Fletcher had been trying to find that pirate for years; he was a tricky bastard. But if he had help...well, he might be successful.

"You don't have to do that," Fletcher finally said. These were his demons—he didn't want anyone else sacrificing themselves to slay them.

"I want to," Nona implored.

"I do, too," Lars said.

Fletcher looked between the two, stunned that they were volunteering for such a mission. Time off was rare, and to offer theirs up to hunt down a dangerous pirate wasn't something they'd do just for their XO. It was a sacrifice one would make for a friend.

13

Hatch's Lab, *Ricky Bobby*, Tangki System

"When do you think it will be operational?" Eddie asked Liesel, studying the blueprints in front of him.

"It's hard to say," she reasoned, toggling her head back and forth. "I've got a few ship repairs that are taking priority, so I can only work on this in my spare time."

"So I'm guessing asking for you to build a pool with a slide on the third deck is out of the question?" Eddie pretended to ask.

Liesel fidgeted with her necklace, made of lug nuts. "This ship does need a water element of some sort. I could draw up plans for a fountain."

Eddie shook his head. "I can't dive into a fountain."

"I'll see if I can come up with something else that suits you," Liesel said. "Currently, we have three of the five elements represented on the ship, which is important for achieving balance."

"Elements?" Julianna asked as she and Hatch approached.

"Yes, the fire, air and earth elements are all represented on *Ricky Bobby*," Liesel explained.

Eddie cut his eyes at Hatch, fairly sure the mechanic would tear Liesel in half for this kind of hippie talk.

"What is the fifth element?" Hatch asked.

"Spirit, of course," the engineer said with a light laugh.

Eddie chuckled. "Come on, Hatch. How did you not know that?"

Hatch puffed up his cheeks. "Teach, I've had about enough of you."

"What are you talking about?" Eddie complained. "I haven't seen you in days,"

"Has it only been a few days?" Hatch asked.

"So after we have the Wiccan shrine constructed, then we're getting a pool, right?" Pip asked through the overhead speaker.

Liesel laughed. "Not Wiccan. But I do think having a meditation area with candles and an intention wall would be really nice."

Again Eddie expected Hatch to grimace, or at least flush from embarrassment. There was no doubt that Liesel was an incredibly talented and efficient engineer, but she'd been Hatch's choice, and her oddities reflected on him.

Instead, Hatch pointed a tentacle at the blueprints resting on the station. "I'm still skeptical about the legitimacy of this project."

"It's only a weapon that we have at our disposal," Eddie

stated. "Just because we have it doesn't mean we have to use it. Jules and I discussed it at length, and we think it's better to have it and not use it than to not have the option at all. Isn't that right?"

Julianna peered around the lab, seemingly distracted.

"Jules, isn't that right?" Eddie asked again.

She startled, looking around at them. "Huh? Yeah, we need options."

"Where's your head?" Eddie asked.

Julianna cleared her throat, stepping around to peer behind a shelf. "It's nothing. I'm looking for something... well, someone."

"Knox isn't here," Hatch told her. "I gave him the day off. Actually, I told him he was fired."

"Hatch!" Julianna reprimanded.

"What?" Hatch threw up two tentacles. "He's stressed and needs to get some rest, but every time I offer him time off, he refuses."

"So you fired him?" Liesel asked, looking amused.

"I'll rehire him tomorrow." Hatch waved them off.

"But in the meantime, he's probably pretty upset," Eddie said.

"He's upset anyway," Hatch complained. "At least he can try and get some rest this way."

"Your management style is interesting," the captain observed.

"You probably don't get it, since I don't encourage my direct subordinates to get plastered," Hatch quipped.

Julianna was back to searching the lab, Eddie noticed.

"Who are you looking for?" he asked.

She tensed. "Marilla mentioned that Harley has been missing since he ran off after Sebastian."

"Oh, that's strange," Eddie said, turning in a circle, looking for the dog.

"'Bastian?" Liesel called. The ferret popped his head out of a can in the supply area of the lab.

"Dammit, you better not be organizing my parts again, rodent!" Hatch yelled, his face flushing pink.

The ferret scurried over to Liesel, crawling up her pants and shirtfront until he was on her shoulder.

"You're not creating trouble for the doctor, are you?" she asked the ferret.

Sebastian clucked and sniffed.

"I can't find a damn thing since he was in here last," Hatch complained.

"My apologies," Liesel said sincerely.

"It's fine. It's fine." Hatch turned, waddling over to a nearby workstation.

"Have you seen Harley?" Liesel asked the ferret.

"I don't think he's going to answer you," Julianna said, giving Liesel a quizzical expression. "Ricky Bobby, do you have any information on the dog?"

"I'm currently conducting a complete scan of the ship to try and locate him," Ricky Bobby stated.

"Have you checked the cargo bay?" Liesel asked, Sebastian clicking loudly in her ear.

"My records show that was the last place the dog was seen," Ricky Bobby reported.

Eddie gave Liesel and her ferret a long look of disbelief. "Bizarre," he said in a hush.

"Let us know when you locate him," Julianna ordered.

"It's possible that he's in one of the compartments I don't have the ability to monitor," Ricky Bobby suggested.

Julianna nodded. "Maybe I should go down there and look for him."

Hatch spun around, holding the Saverus goggles. "You, Julie, are the commander of this ship. Do you think it wise for you to spend your time searching the cargo bay for a canine?"

"I...I'm only worried about Harley for Marilla," Julianna stuttered. "He's her dog, and she's our comms officer."

"Then maybe Marilla should be searching for her dog," Hatch countered.

Julianna couldn't admit that Harley quit being Marilla's dog as soon as he met *her*.

Those two had a bond that even Eddie didn't understand, but he read the worry in her eyes.

"Yeah, you're right," Julianna said, jogging for the exit. "I'll tell her where to look."

"I can relay the message, if you'd like," Ricky Bobby offered.

Julianna was already gone.

Hatch held up the Saverus goggles. "I guess she's not interested in hearing my news, then."

"The goggles are ready?" Eddie guessed.

"No, it's my birthday, you idiot," Hatch said, his eyes narrowed. "Hell yes, the goggles are complete."

"Good news!" Eddie sang.

"Well, don't celebrate yet," Hatch said, his tone flat. "They still need to be tested, which is your damn job."

"Which means I have the privilege of paying our prisoner a visit." Eddie sighed with dread. That Saverus had a way of fucking with his head.

14

Planet L2SCQ-6 in Frontier space

The council was finally taking Verdok seriously. He'd failed before. He hadn't progressed as fast as they would have liked. But without him then they wouldn't have a lead and the elders knew it. More importantly, he was one step ahead of Ghost Squadron. They were still camped on Nexus when he'd taken off for Planet L2SCQ-6.

Before Verdok had to work with Penrae who messed up every single mission. He'd proven his worth though and now he had three skilled members from the council working for him. He turned, slithering in front of the others. The fleet had sent these council members over that morning. They were skilled at shapeshifting, which was key to succeeding in this mission with Ghost Squadron closing in on them.

"Tell me what you learned on your expedition," Verdok ordered, turning to face the three.

The first, a Saverus who passed the ritual test only recently, swayed, his tongue flicking from his mouth. "I scoured the eastern side and learned that a boy with a Mohawk was taken in by a mechanic. A man who ran the Defiance Trading Company."

"That's progress," Verdok said. "Where is this man now?"

"He's dead," the Saverus stated.

"What else?" Verdok asked, turning to the other two.

The one in the middle shrunk back, obviously not having any information of use.

"I asked around about the crash and discovered something interesting," the Saverus on the end said.

"Go on then," Verdok encouraged.

"It happened next to a junkyard," the Saverus imparted.

"Why is that of use?" Verdok asked.

"Because, you said that the boy was thought to be dead," the Saverus stated. "If the authorities didn't think there were any survivors, it's because the boy ran off before they could find him."

"And?" Verdok asked, his tone growing impatient.

"And, if you're a scared child, maybe you'd try and find a place to hide after crashing on a foreign planet," the Saverus said.

"Oh..." Verdok mused on the idea. "Yes, the junkyard would make a perfect place to hide, both a child and the Tangle Thief."

. . .

Brig, *Ricky Bobby*, Tangki System

As soon as Eddie entered the Brig, the fucking Saverus had shifted. She'd taken the form of Harley, which at the moment was a cruel joke since the dog was missing.

"Your game is about to be up," Eddie threatened, pressing the goggles to his face and pulling the strap securely around the back of his head. He adjusted them until they were in place. The Saverus goggles were pretty weighty, forcing his chin down. Eddie had to work to keep them balanced, which meant they wouldn't be something he could wear in battle.

The Saverus shifted into the form of Julianna. She turned, brushing her ass across the bars, shaking her hips. "You like what you see, big boy? Bars aren't poles, but I can still dance around them."

Julianna would skin this fucking "See you next Tuesday" if she saw this.

Eddie did his best to ignore the imposter form of Julianna as she grinded against the bars. He tried to remember what Hatch had said about the settings. *Turn the lens to the right while staring at a shapeshifted Saverus.*

No problem, he thought.

The fake Julianna grabbed the bars with both hands, throwing her head back and arching her spine.

Eddie willed himself to focus and turned the lens once.

Nothing happened.

"You look like you could use a lap dance," the Saverus said in Julianna's voice.

Eddie turned the lens again.

Nothing.

"Open up this cell and I'll give you a show," imposter Julianna said. "No one needs to know."

Eddie turned the lens again.

Again there was no change.

Damnit, there was only one more setting left.

"I see the way you look at your partner," the Saverus said. "I can be her for a night. I promise you that I'll feel the same."

Revulsion rose up in Eddie's throat as he turned the lens one last time. The image of Julianna dancing against the bars was replaced with the form of the giant red snake with bright green eyes. Her tongue flicked out her mouth as she swayed behind the bars.

A laugh burst out of Eddie's mouth. "I don't fuck snakes, which is exactly what you look like to me."

The Saverus halted, its head sinking back a few inches. "Those goggles? Do they…"

Eddie nodded, holding the goggles in place. "That's right. I can see you in your pure, scaly form."

"Oh…"

"Which means your mind-fuck games aren't going to work anymore," Eddie said triumphantly.

"Okay okay," the Saverus said in a rush. "I'm willing to cooperate."

Eddie smiled. "About damn time."

"What do you want to know?" the Saverus asked. With the goggles on, Eddie could see exactly how fearful the snake was.

"Why don't you start by telling me what the Saverus want the Tangle Thief for?" Eddie asked.

The snake shook her head. "I don't know."

"Don't lie."

"I'm not," the Saverus said with a hiss. "The council wouldn't tell someone like me such a thing. It was only my job, along with my partner Verdok, to get the Tangle Thief."

Well, at least they were getting somewhere. This was progress. "Verdok? That's the other Saverus that got away?"

"Yes, and he left me for dead," the Saverus said bitterly.

Eddie laughed morbidly. "Not only that, but he fucking used you as a shield."

The Saverus's green eyes narrowed. "I remember."

"And Verdok, is probably out there right now, trying to beat us to the Tangle Thief," Eddie stated. That Saverus knew that Knox had been transported to a safe place on Nexus. He'd obviously figured out that was Sunex and had sent the Petigrens there. Eddie had to hope that this Verdok hadn't learned what they had: that Knox took the Tangle Thief to Planet L2SCQ-6.

"I can tell you exactly where Verdok is," the Saverus stated.

Eddie lifted a curious eyebrow. "Don't fuck with me, snake."

"My partner left me for dead. I think you should go after him so he can share a cell with me," the Saverus said.

"How will that benefit us?" Eddie asked.

"He'll have the newest lead on the Tangle Thief," the

Saverus explained. "Take him out and you'll have one less obstacle to getting to the device before my council."

"How do you know where Verdok is?"

"Because he was my partner," she said.

Eddie lowered the goggles, the image of Julianna not having the same effect on him now that the illusion was broken. "Fine, give me the coordinates."

15

Bridge, *Ricky Bobby*, Tangki System

Eddie and Julianna stood on the bridge watching the view screen. "Gate into Alchon System has been created. We will jump on your command," Ricky Bobby informed them.

Julianna pulled her gaze away from the radar screen. "Verdok's ship will be at these coordinates?" she asked Eddie for the fifth time. Trusting a Saverus wasn't an easy thing to do, but not taking the information felt as foolish.

Eddie chewed on the inside of his cheek, hesitation written in his eyes. "Yes, but according to the prisoner, he's stationed in a dropship. *Ricky Bobby* can tear him ten new assholes."

Julianna nodded, but something felt off about this. Maybe it was venturing into a foreign system. They'd discussed gating on the far side of a distant moon and taking the Q-Ships to Verdok's location, but the problem with that was the many asteroid belts that posed navigational challenges.

Delaying the action, though, felt like inevitable defeat. Julianna eyed Eddie, a confirmation heavy in his gaze.

"Ricky Bobby, jump now," Julianna commanded.

"Initiating sequence," the AI confirmed. "Gating commencing in five, four, three, two…one."

Julianna's head tightened, and her mouth felt instantly dry. Blackness. She thought she'd be used to it by now, but it wasn't a natural experience for her, and the sensations were never the same when gating.

"Jump complete," Ricky Bobby said.

"Report," Julianna demanded, blinking at the radar, waiting for the system to come back online.

"Cloaks are down," Ricky Bobby stated. "There's a radiation field in this system that's knocked them out."

"Get Liesel on a fix, pronto," Eddie said.

On the radar, a battlecruiser twice the size of *Ricky Bobby* materialized.

"Fuck!" Julianna jumped. "That's no dropship."

Ships blinked into view on the radar all around *Ricky Bobby*.

"We've dropped into a motherfucking fleet!" Eddie yelled.

Around them on the bridge, the comms officers were typing furiously. One darted back and forth between stations, searching for intel on the sixteen ships that were now surrounding them.

"Who are they?" Julianna asked.

"I'm not finding any identification," Ricky Bobby stated.

"I've tried establishing a connection with the main ship, but there's no answer," one of the comms officers informed them.

Eddie scratched his chin nervously. "Friendly ships usually reply."

"There's no reason to jump to conclusions," Julianna said.

"A missile has been launched from the main ship," Ricky Bobby said matter-of-factly.

"Fuck!" Eddie yelled. "Can I jump to conclusions now?"

"Can we jump?" Julianna asked.

"Gate engines are still discharged. They need time to recharge," Ricky Bobby reported.

"Can we dodge it?" Eddie asked.

"We can out-maneuver most of the fleet, except for the main battlecruiser," Ricky Bobby stated.

Julianna pressed her fingers to her mouth, thinking. "How are shields?"

"They will hold against this missile, which will impact in fifteen seconds," Ricky Bobby said.

"How much more can we take?" Julianna asked.

"If they launch nuclear weapons, we are done," Ricky Bobby said.

"Deploy Black Eagles," Eddie ordered. "We need to put up a fight until engines are ready. How long will that take?"

"Six minutes," Ricky Bobby informed them.

Eddie gave Julianna a worried stare. "Those are going to be the longest fucking six minutes of my life."

"I'm not sure how this is possible," one of the comms

officers said over the commotion. Everyone on the bridge was hustling, surfing through intel.

Fletcher ran over to the officer's workstation. He squinted at the screen.

"What is it?" Julianna asked.

"Battlecruiser has deployed single flyers," Ricky Bobby interjected.

Fletcher jerked his head up. "She's found a connection between one of the ships in the fleet, and one from a back-logged database."

"Get to the point," Eddie demanded, his tone urgent.

"This particular ship was created on the planet of Savern," Fletcher stated.

"Are you implying...?" Julianna's heart was pounding hard in her chest.

The cold look in Fletcher's eyes answered her question before his voice did. "We might have jumped into the Saverus's fleet."

"That damn bitch!" Eddie yelled. *This is my fault; I shouldn't have trusted the prisoner.*

"I can confirm that the ship in question was produced on Savern," Ricky Bobby stated. "The other ships have no identification, but I'm running a scan for a connection between the weapons and Savern, as well as trying to establish contact with them."

"The Saverus have been hiding for centuries," Julianna

reasoned. "Of course they wouldn't want their ships to identify them."

"Ricky Bobby," Eddie began. "In your communication to the fleet, tell them we have one of their own aboard, and that we will release her to them if they cease fire."

"Sending communication now," Ricky Bobby confirmed.

"Carnivore here," Lars said over the comms. "These guys aren't playing around. They are hitting us with everything they have."

Eddie scanned the radar. "Damn, they have a lot of flyers. We're going to be overwhelmed in no time."

"Can you identify their supply ship?" Julianna asked.

"Yes," Ricky Bobby said simply.

"Deploy missiles," Julianna ordered. "Take it the fuck out. They need to know that we mean business."

"Good thinking," Eddie said.

"Ricky Bobby, have you heard a reply regarding exchanging the hostage?" Julianna asked.

"Negative," Ricky Bobby answered. "The communication went through, but they aren't responding."

"I'll take that as a 'no', then," Julianna said.

"How are we going to hold them off?" Eddie asked.

Julianna drew in a breath. "One of us needs to get out there in the Q-Ship. A cloaked ship can offer the protection Ricky Bobby needs."

Eddie was running for the exit before Julianna finished her sentence.

Lars rolled out of the trajectory of enemy fire. *These bastards are aggressive.* Their single flyers were covered in chrome, and kept blinding him with a strange glare as they passed.

"I've got two fuckers on my tail I can't shake," Lone Wolf called out over the comm.

Lars glanced at the radar, which was covered in a mess of dots. He'd never been in the thick of a fleet like this. "Carnivore coming to the rescue."

Redirecting, Lars slid his ship between two of the chrome flyers before they could block his path. He caught sight of Lone Wolf and the two enemies trailing him; his squadmate was right, they were expert flyers, not giving him a breath of space. For whatever reason, though, they weren't firing.

Lars locked onto one, waiting until he'd closed the distance before firing. The chrome ship sparkled, momentarily playing with his vision. Suddenly, the two ships trailing Lone Wolf shifted, morphing into Black Eagles.

"MY GOD!" Lars yelled.

"What the fuck?" Lone Wolf gasped.

"What's going on?" Julianna asked over the comm.

Lars twisted his ship around. All of the chrome ships had disappeared, and he was in a sea of Black Eagles.

"Are you fucking with me?" Julianna pressed her head into her hand.

"All the enemy ships have morphed into Black Eagles," Lars repeated.

"Ricky Bobby, is there any way to distinguish our own on the radar?" Julianna asked.

"Of course. Each Black Eagle is chipped and ready to squawk in combat mode four, but it will take me a moment to remotely activate their systems," Ricky Bobby said.

"Black Beard, are you out there?" Julianna asked, hoping that Eddie hadn't launched the Q-Ship. She realized her idea had been a bad one.

There was a pause.

"Yes, Strong Arm, flying into position," Eddie finally reported.

Julianna let out a hot breath. "No ships can return to *Ricky Bobby* until you're actively squawking mode four."

"Why would I want to return before having a little fun?" Eddie asked, his voice light from his joy of flying.

"You aren't out there yet, are you, Black Beard?" Lars asked over the comm.

"Oh, fuck," Eddie said in a hush. "Their ships can shapeshift."

"It would appear," Julianna said dryly. *I am going to strangle that damn Saverus in the brig if we survive this.*

"Another missile has been launched and is headed straight for the bow," Ricky Bobby said.

"Can you maneuver to avoid it?" Julianna asked.

"I can divert it for up to ten seconds," he replied.

"I'm on it," Eddie chimed in. "That missile is mine."

The sea of Black Eagles, most of them not belonging to Ghost Squadron, was a trip to see. However, that wasn't Eddie's present concern.

He locked his controls onto the missile that had missed the bow of *Ricky Bobby*.

The missile swerved, turning around to make another attempt.

"Oh, no you don't!" Eddie yelled, initiating his own attack, a single canon.

He banked the Q-Ship hard to the side to avoid the blast impacts from enemy ships.

Ricky Bobby would take damage, but not as much as it would if the missile had hit directly.

"They've fired two more missiles," Julianna reported over the comm.

"Fuck these guys," Eddie said, tumbling the ship down and around, making a quick turn.

"Missiles headed for starboard. Can you intercept?" Julianna asked.

Eddie blinked at the new sight in front of him, unsure for a moment exactly what he was seeing.

"Black Beard?" Julianna barked.

"Yeah, I'm here," Eddie said, momentarily dumbstruck.

"Can you take out the missiles?"

"If I can figure out which ship is *Ricky Bobby*," Eddie stated.

He was on the back end of the fleet, and every large ship had shifted, taking on the appearance of *Ricky Bobby*.

"How is that possible?" Julianna asked, scanning the radar. There was no distinction between her ships and those of the Saverus fleet.

"Should I question the prisoner?" Fletcher asked.

Julianna shook her head. "That bitch isn't telling us anything useful."

"Shields won't hold much longer," Ricky Bobby said.

"Position the ship so that the next missile hits the brig," she commanded. "I want that fucking Saverus to feel the attacks of her own kind. If this ship is going down, she's getting taken out first."

"We're trapped out here!" Lars yelled over the comm. "We can only shoot at the ones shooting at us, which means we're constantly on the defense."

"Ricky Bobby, when will the transponders be active?" Julianna asked.

"I'm uploading an update now," Ricky Bobby said. "Give me ten seconds."

"And the gate engine?"

She hated that they were so vulnerable. *How did we get into this?*

"It is almost completely charged. One-minute remaining," Ricky Bobby answered.

The ship rocked, and Fletcher stumbled forward into the radar screen.

Julianna tightened her eyes on the radar as it blinked twice. A moment later, the monochrome scan was replaced with blue and red dots. There were significantly more red ones, and they had the larger ships.

"Radar updated," Julianna called over the comm. "All of

you, return *now*!"

"Roger that, Strong Arm," Eddie said, his tone heavy.

Fletcher leaned in closer to the radar. "I'll make sure none of the Saverus get in."

"Good, one infestation, and we will be fucking screwed," Julianna said.

Ricky Bobby took another blow, making the lights flicker and then go out completely. The generator kicked on immediately, bathing the bridge in soft blue light.

"Gate engines delayed due to system outage," Ricky Bobby said.

Julianna gripped the table until her knuckles turned white. "We're fucking sitting ducks."

"Should we deploy more missiles?" Fletcher asked.

Julianna shook her head. "It will only drain our systems. We need to jump. There's no winning this battle."

She hated having to run, but knowing when an enemy had you beat was crucial. It was always better to survive to fight another day, especially in the face of such overwhelming odds. If they got out of this, they could return to deliver the Saverus their own asses. With proper strategizing, Julianna was sure *Ricky Bobby* could take them out; it was being dropped unprepared into a giant fleet, that had been their shortcoming.

"Gate engines charged and ready to go," Ricky Bobby said.

"Black Eagles? Black Beard? Are you back?" Julianna asked over the comm.

"I'm the last," Eddie said. "Landing now."

"Ricky Bobby, jump now!" Julianna ordered.

16

Lower Deck, *Ricky Bobby*, Tangki System

Steam billowed from the rafters overhead. Three crew members were fighting an electrical fire at the end of the corridor. Loud banging echoed from inside the walls of the ship. *Ricky Bobby* was in chaos.

"Diagnostics report the ship is at forty-three percent," Liesel said, scrolling through the results.

"Fuck, we took a huge hit," Eddie said, sliding his hand through his hair.

"Well guess who else is going to?" Julianna said, staring around at the aftermath of the attack.

"Later. Most importantly, we need cloaks online," Eddie stated.

Liesel widened her eyes before looking up. "Shields are also down."

"Okay, second most important," Eddied corrected. "We need those shields back up immediately."

"I doubt the Saverus followed," Julianna stated.

Eddie nodded. "I agree, but I'd feel more comfortable if we were prepared for another attack."

"How is the new weapon coming along?" Julianna asked.

Liesel swiped through several screens before replying, "It's almost complete, but I'm going to have to put it on hold."

Eddie gave a low whistle. "That would have obliterated them."

"Put the project on Hatch's plate," Julianna said. "We need a weapon in case we have another run-in with the Saverus; nothing we have right now will defeat them."

Eddie looked at her with a skeptical reluctance. "I don't think you would have authorized using that weapon when there were other options at our disposal."

"We were the ones nearly disposed of, so don't be so sure."

Julianna was mad. No, she was fucking *livid*. They hadn't stood a chance against the Saverus; their ships could shapeshift. It made her realize exactly how powerful this alien race could be.

"How about you take this hostility out on our prisoner?" Eddie asked, leading her down the corridor.

Julianna was about to answer when Ricky Bobby cut her off. "I've found the dog named Harley."

"What? Where?" Julianna's pulse quickened.

"He's not far from here," the AI assured her. "I was right; he was in the cargo bay. It appears that he burrowed into one of the vent tunnels."

Julianna let out a weighty breath. "Dumb dog was intent on finding that damn ferret."

"It would appear," Eddie said with a laugh.

"Where is he now?" the commander asked. *I'm going to ignore him for a week for pulling this stunt.*

"He's in the vent tunnel, down this corridor on the right," Ricky Bobby said.

Julianna hurried in the given direction. *The damn dog is probably cowering in the tunnel, knowing he's about to get chewed out.*

"The section of the vent where Harley is located suffered one of the biggest impacts during the battle," Ricky Bobby said.

Julianna slowed. Paused. Turned to read the apprehension on Eddie's face. "What? What does that mean?"

"Is he alive?" Eddie asked tensely, watching Jules.

"I believe so," Ricky Bobby replied, "but he's not moving. The vent where he's located appears to have been crushed."

"Fuck!" Julianna yelled, running. "We have to get him out."

Eddie was on her heels. "How are we going to do that?"

Julianna pulled the grate up off the vent. She kneeled, peering into the fifteen-by-fifteen-inch space. Without hesitating, Julianna slithered into the tunnel.

"Are you crazy?" Eddie asked, crouching on the ground beside her.

"No, I'm problem solving!" The metal tunnel was cold and smelled of mold and dust.

"You're going to get stuck in there!" Eddie yelled.

"Are you calling me fat?"

She immediately regretted yelling. Her voice echoed off the metal, making her ears ring. She couldn't see a damn thing in the darkened tunnel. "Hand me a flashlight," Julianna said, squeezing her hand behind her and combing her fingers in Eddie's direction.

"Damn it, Jules," Eddie said, searching his belt. "There could be a fire or any kind of damage in there. You have no idea what you're getting yourself into."

"Eddie, flashlight! Now!"

"Here!"

Something cold was slapped into Julianna's hand. She negotiated her arm back in front of her, scratching her skin on the seams of the metal encasing her.

When she turned on the flashlight, her heart sank. "Fuck," she sighed.

"What is it? Did you find him?" Eddie asked from by her feet.

Julianna began to inch her way down the tunnel, toward the dog's ass, which was most of what she could make out, twenty feet away.

"Yes. He's on his side and looks to be pinned where the tunnel caved in overhead," Julianna explained. Her progress was slow, but considering she had an inch of room between her and the tunnel, her speed was fairly good.

"Ricky Bobby scanned that area," Eddie called in to her. "That whole section is unstable, and likely to cave from pressure overhead."

"So I'll be fast," Julianna muttered in response.

"Fuck, Jules!" Eddie growled.

You're risking your life for an animal again.

So?

So, you're starting to get a reputation.

For being an idiot?

For having a heart.

That's inherently false. I'm only bored. That's why I'm doing this.

It isn't because you love that dog?

Right now, I despise that dog.

So you're risking your life to save him?

I can't have the mutt clogging up the vents.

Liesel is in charge of ship maintenance. Shouldn't she be the one on this?

I'm already in here, and she's probably not strong enough to do what's got to be done to get Harley out.

And what's got to be done?

I've got no fucking clue. I'll figure it out, though.

Harley whimpered as Julianna approached. Between the caving metal, Julianna spied his face as he tried to curl up to look at her. When he moved, he yelped in pain, echoing loudly in the tunnel. The entire section shifted, and the metal pinning him slid further into his ribcage.

"What's going on?" Eddie called.

"It's okay," Julianna called to Harley, her voice soft. "I'm going to get you out of here."

She struggled to pull a full breath into her lungs. The clogged section of the vent had little fresh air.

Harley whimpered again.

It tore at the heart Julianna didn't think she had. *What is*

157

*happening to me lately? I seem to...**care**—and more than about the greater good or the Federation. I care about this dog, and my team, and, if I'm honest with myself, Eddie.*

Fuck my life.

I heard that.

The 'fuck my life' part?

The caring part.

Like I said, fuck my life.

When Julianna was close enough, she reached out for the metal protruding into Harley's back end.

He snapped at her, then emitted a soft, regretful growl, low in his throat.

"Hey, I'm trying to help," Julianna scolded.

From the other side of the metal, Julianna spied the look of remorse on Harley's face.

He's in pain and scared. That's what animals and children do when they're afraid. They react. They snap at those trying to help.

She sighed. *Dammit. How am I going to get him out?*

The tunnel shook. Julianna threw her hand out, holding up the metal section that had fallen into Harley to keep it from stabbing more deeply into his flesh.

If you're not too busy...

This is about the worst time ever, Julianna replied, trying to push the metal section up. Harley growled, nipping at her.

I can sense that, but I thought you should know that the vent tunnel isn't going to hold much longer.

You're a dear. Thanks for the info.

I'm not done providing sage wisdom.

Is that what you're doing? Julianna punched into the metal, trying force it back up and meeting defeat again. "Dammit!" she shouted out in frustration.

According to the blueprints for the ship, on the other side of Harley, there is an access door that leads to the floor below you.

On the other side of the dog.

Yes, you're listening. Great.

The dog who I can't free, nor get around.

The broken metal of the vent was wedged so firmly into Harley's side that Julianna thought she'd have to retreat and have him cut out. She didn't know if he had that kind of time.

What if you pushed him forward, over the access vent? Pip asked.

Julianna was about to argue, but paused.

Pip, that's actually a really good idea.

I'm full of them, you'll find.

Work on the modesty, though.

She was having zero luck with trying to push the metal that was pinning Harley out of the way. Urging the dog forward would hurt him a great deal, but it could possibly free him from the stuck metal.

Securing her hands on Harley's back end, Julianna pressed her toes and elbows underneath her. She'd have to push swiftly, to clear him of the space and minimize his wounds.

You can do this, Pip encouraged.

I can't tell you how much I need to hear that right now. Julianna gritted down hard on her teeth.

I know.

Julianna drew in a breath. On the exhale she pressed her arms straight, pushing Harley.

He snapped at her, letting out another yelp.

"I know. I know," Julianna said through a grunt.

The broken piece of the tunnel released and Julianna knocked it hard. She unleashed a great deal of strength forcing the broken section of the vent back. Now that Harley was out of the way and she didn't have to worry about harming him she could push her limits. With the vent cleared, Julianna spied the giant laceration from Harley's spine to the middle of his stomach.

His insides spilled out, and he roared with fearful pain.

Julianna gritted her teeth, blocking out the desperate whimpering of the dog. She forced harder, pushing up onto her knees and bolting forward.

The grate of the access door pinched her legs.

"Fucking hell!" Julianna rejoiced, pushing once more. She knew that every movement was endangering Harley, but she had to get him out of there.

The tunnel shifted, dropping down a foot and leaning to the side. Julianna kicked her heel into the access door once. Twice. On the third time, the grate fell, clattering to the ground.

"Tell Eddie that I'm—"

"Julianna! Is that you?" Eddie's voice called underneath her.

On it! Pip exclaimed.

Thanks.

Julianna grabbed onto Harley, careful to hold him in a

way that didn't put more stress on his wounds. She pushed her legs out of the access area and felt hands wrap around them. Eddie lowered her to the ground, and Julianna looked up at him. Her mouth fell open but nothing came out.

Eddie's eyes shot to Harley in her arms. "Is he—"

A loud groan stole their attention. The vent dropped several inches, bolts flying off in different directions. Eddie yanked both Julianna and Harley to the side.

Julianna continued moving forward, getting as far as she could from the duct before it crashed to the ground. She didn't stop when they were in the clear.

"Where are you going?" Eddie asked, running beside her. "The infirmary is the opposite direction."

"The doctors can't save him," Julianna said, pressing Harley firmer into her chest.

They were both covered in his blood. His eyes were closed, but she felt his heart still beating.

"The Pod-doc?" Eddie asked.

"It's his only chance." Julianna sped up, knowing they were running out of time.

17

Hatch's Lab, *Ricky Bobby*, Tangki System

"I don't know," Pip said, a laugh in his tone, "*I* think she's kind of pretty."

"Pretty? I haven't noticed," Hatch said, spinning a wrench in one of his tentacles.

"Oh, really?" Pip challenged. "Then why is that every time Liesel comes around, your temperature rises and your eight hearts beat faster?"

Hatch puffed out his cheeks. "What? They do not."

"I can upload your stats for you to review, if you don't believe me," the AI teased.

Hatch gave Knox a pointed stare that was meant for Pip. "I think that interfacing you with the lab was a bad idea. It's obvious that you're more of a distraction than an assistant."

"Not to mention that my observations regarding Liesel are challenging something that you're in deep denial about," Pip said.

He doesn't know when to stop, Hatch thought. *And to think that Julie has to put up with him full-time... She must have unending patience.*

"I can totally get it," Pip continued. "She's smart, really pretty, has a spunk that you find interesting, and she's—"

"Pip!" Hatch yelled, startling Knox.

Ignoring him, Pip said, "She's not my type, if you must know. I prefer my ladies a little taller. Oh, and I love brunettes. Who says they aren't as much fun as blondes? But you obviously have a thing for the pixie types, which I can respect."

"That's quite enough!" Hatch's head felt like it was about to explode. He had half a mind to downgrade Pip's programming, turn him into an EI.

"Oh, don't get so excited," Pip chortled. "I'm not implying anything is going on between you two. I mean, the anatomical conundrum that a human and Londil pairing poses is beyond my capacity to sort out. I'm only strongly suggesting that you have a little crush, which is completely normal for a Londil of your age when going through a mid-life crisis."

Hatch flung a wrench across the lab, throwing most of his tentacles above his head. It wasn't that he was attracted to Liesel. He didn't actually know what got to him about her.

"I DO NOT like Liesel!" Hatch yelled, turning to leave the lab and escape the taunting.

Hatch's eyes widened. His mouth fell open. His eight hearts palpitated.

Standing squarely in the entrance to his lab was Liesel Magner, a look of utter heartbreak on her face.

"Uhhh...L-L-Liesel!" Hatch stammered.

"Wow, this is a little uncomfortable," Pip said in a squeaky voice. "I think I hear Julianna calling me. Gotta go!"

The chief engineer drew herself up, lifting her chin. She reached down and picked up the wrench that Hatch had thrown across the room. "If you didn't like me before, then you're going to fully hate me now."

"Liesel, it's not like that," Hatch said in rush. "Pip was provoking me."

She shook her head, a pleasant smile now on her face. "It's fine. I heard you clearly; although I'm sad about it, I know I can't make anyone like me."

"Pip was making it sound like Hatch had a crush on you," Knox cut in.

Hatch closed his eyes for a beat, wishing he could disappear. He shook his head, looking at Knox. "Gunner, stay out of this."

"I was trying to help," Knox explained, looking between Hatch and Liesel. "It's all a big misunderstanding."

"Hey, Gunner, you know how I rehired you this morning?" Hatch asked.

"Y-y-yeah," Knox stuttered.

"Well, you're fired...again. Clear out." Hatch pointed at the exit.

Knox didn't argue. Hopefully he knew that tomorrow he'd be rehired; Hatch needed space today.

Dropping his tool on the workstation, Knox headed for the exit. Liesel gave him a sympathetic look as he passed.

Hatch knew he was being cruel, but he couldn't stop himself. Maybe it was the midlife crisis comment. Hatch wasn't getting enhancements to his tentacles, or dyeing his skin like most Londils did when growing older...

The baby blue Mustang 390GT he'd been working on caught his eye; the muscle cars *were* taking over his lab lately. Maybe he was "going through something," but it was definitely none of Pip's or anyone else's business.

"You really like your apprentice," Liesel observed when they were alone.

"I like you, too...professionally," Hatch said, adding the last part a beat later.

"And I hold only the highest level of respect for you," Liesel said. "But Knox means a lot to you. He represents a part of yourself."

"He's a kid I'm teaching." Hatch shook his head, waddling back to his main workstation.

"He's the next generation of mechanics," Liesel pressed.

"What does that have to do with anything?" *I don't have time for this.* He'd only completed one pair of the Saverus goggles, and finishing another one would take time, especially because he kept firing Knox.

"Evolution is a healthy part of us and the organization that we're a part of," Liesel said.

"And?"

"And it can also challenge us," Liesel continued.

"I'm not feeling challenged enough," Hatch declared. "Maybe that's the problem."

"Maybe," Liesel said, her voice doubtful. "I think it's more likely that you're afraid of what will happen to you as Ghost Squadron continues to evolve. Will there always be a place for Doctor A'Din Hatcherik? That place is surely going to change; it already has. Now you have a chief engineer you have to answer to. I don't think you dislike me so much as I make you nervous because of what I represent."

Hatch's face pinched with confused outrage. "I don't have to answer to you."

Liesel wasn't deterred, only continuing to smile at him. "I would think that, on this ship, we all answer to each other. That's how a team works."

"This is ridiculous. And what do you mean by what you represent?" Hatch asked, his breath hot.

"I represent the change. Before I was hired, you had full control over all the projects on the ship. And control is something I think you crave," Liesel said casually.

Hatch's cheeks were burning hot with anger. He shook off the ridiculous notion. "Why are you here?"

Liesel released a clever smile. "Why am I here? What are any of us doing here? It's the grandest question."

"Oh, stop with your hippie bullshit!"

"Fine." Liesel pulled a pad from the holder on her waist, handing it to Hatch. "I'm specifically here because the captain and commander want you to take over on this project, since I need to focus on ship repairs."

Hatch took the pad, a sound of frustration falling from his mouth. "You're not serious? I'm supposed to take over building the weapon?"

Liesel shrugged weakly. "I prefer to call it the 'leveling

laser' rather than 'weapon'."

"It's a weapon," Hatch argued.

"A bulldozer isn't considered a weapon, but it does something similar."

"I don't like that you play this semantic bullshit with me."

Liesel dared to smile sweetly. "I completely understand that me assigning you this project makes things tense. I know how you feel about the leveling laser."

She is either the dumbest person in the galaxy, or she has a death wish. "You're not assigning me anything!" Hatch roared.

"No, you're right. This order came from the captain and commander, like I mentioned."

"Fine, I'll do it—but only because we were nearly demolished by an alien race." He glanced at the plans before handing back the pad.

"Do you need me to send these blueprints over to you?" Liesel asked.

"No, I just memorized them."

The chief engineer tilted her head to the side, a calm look of respect on her face. "Okay. Thank you, Dr. A'Din Hatcherik."

"Whatever," Hatch grumbled, putting his back to her.

"Oh, and, Hatch?"

"What?" he barked, opening the hood for the Mustang. He'd get started on the leveling laser soon; first, he needed to calm his nerves.

"Just so you know," Liesel began, "there's no replacing you. Not now. Not ever."

18

Brig, *Ricky Bobby*, Tangki System

"He's going to be okay," Eddie said, watching Julianna pace back and forth in the corridor outside the brig.

Julianna spun around, her hands on her hips. "Who is?"

Eddie's eyes rolled up to the ceiling. "Are you really going to play this off like you're not concerned?"

"I'm not following," Julianna said.

"Jules, you're obviously worried about Harley coming out of the Pod-doc. Will you stop acting so heartless?"

Julianna pulled her gun from her holster. "This isn't an act. I honestly wasn't thinking about Harley just now." She pointed her gun at the door. "My mind was firmly focused on quelling my anger so I don't do something I'll regret. Now why don't you open that door?"

Eddie gave her a discriminating glare, not at all buying her tough-girl act. Jules was tough. The toughest he knew. But she was also human and had feelings. The fact that she was so angry she was resisting the urge to murder a prisoner meant that the attack that nearly killed Harley was burning her up inside.

Eddie placed the goggles onto his face, tightening the band around his head until they were secure. "You sure you don't want the goggles? It does help to break the illusion."

Julianna shook her head. "I don't need them. I know what that *thing* is and can no longer be fooled."

Eddie had never seen Julianna so pissed.

Since he was the one who had taken the coordinates from the Saverus, he figured he'd be the most irate. But Eddie had made the call that he thought was right. There was no going back and changing things. It wasn't that Eddie didn't regret things; it was that he already had one major regret in his life, and everything else paled in comparison.

Yes, the ship got beat up. But no one had died. Even Harley would be okay. In exchange, they'd found the location of the Saverus fleet and learned valuable information about their technology. In his mind, the fuck-up hadn't been completely terrible. There were other decisions that Eddie had made in his life with zero silver lining. *Those* were worth regretting.

Eddie gave Julianna one last look before opening the door to the brig.

The prisoner was in the form of Julianna when they charged into the holding area outside its cell.

Julianna held her pistol steadily at her doppelganger. "Change," she ordered.

The imposter blinked innocently. "Why would you want me to change? I'm you. I'm perfect, don't you think?"

With a precision to impress, Julianna fired her gun, and the bullet grazed the shoulder of her mirror image. The Saverus's hand flew to her shoulder, and her version of Julianna's face was streaked with horror.

"You didn't think I'd shoot at myself, did you?" Julianna asked. "Now change, or you'll feel the next bullet more."

The image of Julianna dissolved into the giant snake, its green eyes blinking impassively. A smear of blood marked its right side where the bullet had grazed.

"You set us up!" Eddie yelled from Julianna's side.

The Saverus dipped its chin, not replying.

Julianna lowered her gun. "You have given us zero factual information, and what little you did tell us nearly got us blown up. There is not much keeping us from throwing you out the airlock."

"Then do it!" the Saverus said with a hiss.

Eddie shook his head, eyes narrowed. "That would show you more kindness than your own race has, including your partner. He used you as a shield and left you behind to be caught."

"Verdok is a vile Saverus. His treatment of me was no surprise," the snake spat, unaffected.

"But your race knows that we have you. We informed them," Julianna said. "And not only have they not tried to rescue you, but when offered your return in exchange for a ceasefire, they declined. They shot at our ship with the intention to destroy. It would appear that they have no concern for your life."

Julianna gave Eddie a sideways look. "Tell me, partner, what would you do if I was captured by the enemy?"

Eddie stepped up closer to the bars, his eyes sharp and centered on the Saverus. "Nothing and no one would stop me from finding you, Jules. I would tear this universe apart to save you."

Julianna smiled inwardly. "And what would Ghost Squadron do if one of ours was on an enemy ship that had jumped within range?"

Eddie laughed hoarsely. "That's easy. We'd negotiate for their release. What we *wouldn't* do is fire at said ship, knowing that we were potentially killing one of our own."

"So you can see how savage that makes your race appear to us," Julianna concluded plainly.

"Our council is very selfish," the snake said. "You wouldn't understand. We are taught selflessness for the good of our kind, and our council takes advantage of that."

"That's an excuse. You're in denial about what's happened here." Julianna stepped even with Eddie, leaning close to the bars. "They have betrayed you. Plain and simple."

"Now you're remaining loyal to a race who would rather see you dead than protect you," Eddie stated.

"It's not like that—"

"Enough!" Julianna stated. "You have one day to decide where your loyalty lies. We've shown you more kindness than your own race, but that will not last. Either you start being of use to us, or we're tossing you out the airlock. No one is going to miss you."

Knox Gunnerson's Private Quarters, *Ricky Bobby*, Tangki System

Consciousness was slow to return to Knox. He felt trapped, but the waking world was a blink away. All he wanted to do was open his eyes. Then his future could begin...one without regret and uncertainty. One where he fixed his problems instead of made them worse.

I have the answers!

The dream was so clear. It was a memory. His memory. It had all come back. Finally, he knew where to look.

If he could only wake from this seemingly unending movie reel of his life, he could tell Julianna and Eddie. They'd be so happy. He'd lost the Tangle Thief—well, hidden it—but now he knew *exactly* where to find it.

It *had* to still be there; he was the only one who knew where it was located. There was no way that anyone else could find it.

Unless they excavated the junkyard... Unless they know exactly where to search and what they are looking for.

His heart beat in his throat. The Saverus were likely to be on his trail. He knew that. Knew it so much, he was afraid he might be too late.

He needed to wake up. If he could jolt himself out of this dream, the beginning of the end could commence.

In his bed, he felt himself toss. The sweat beaded on his

forehead, drenching his pillow. His dry mouth continued to plague him.

Still he stayed locked in dreams.

Wake up! he yelled at his consciousness.

Knox reached for the covers, pulling them to his chest as he shivered. He was so cold. So alone. So tired of fighting.

Why can't I get out of this dream?

In his mind, he screamed so loud that it hurt his ears. So loud that he wanted to escape from himself. So loud that he did wake.

Finally!

Bolting upright in his bed, Knox sat heaving on ragged breath. His covers were tied tightly around his abdomen, and his mattress was soaked. His head was throbbing.

But he didn't care.

He knew exactly where the Tangle Thief was.

19

Landing Bay, *Ricky Bobby*, Tangki System

"A junkyard?" Eddie asked Knox, scratching his head.

"Specifically, a spaceship junkyard on Planet L2SCQ-6," Knox replied.

"From my experience, junkyards tend to be a mess of piled high trash," Julianna cut in. "Do you know exactly where you put the Tangle Thief?"

Knox nodded and then corrected himself, shaking his head. "I know where I hid it, but things could have shifted over the last ten years."

"Or someone could have taken it already," Eddie added.

"As long as it wasn't the Saverus, then we're fine. Whoever took it wouldn't necessarily know how to operate it," Julianna said.

Hatch waddled over, carrying a small, metal case. "Remember that Knox operated the Tangle Thief at age ten. Using the Tangle Thief isn't rocket science."

"Knox is also Cheng's son," Eddie reasoned. "I would assume that his prior experience with technology helped.
"

Hatch puffed out his cheeks. "I'm only saying that it's possible that someone could operate the device."

"But they haven't," Cheng said at Knox's side, his arm protectively wrapping around his son's shoulders at the look of defeat that sprang to his face.

"I hid it really well, I promise," Knox said.

"How do we know that the Tangle Thief hasn't been used over the last ten years?" Julianna asked Cheng.

"Simple," Hatch chirped, handing her the case and waddling away.

Eddie stared down at her, a ghost of a smile on his face. "Well, that explains everything. Hatch can really beat you over the head with an answer, huh?"

Julianna looked again to Cheng, who would be more willing to offer information.

He cleared his throat before saying, "Knox used the Tangle Thief soon after I did, which is why the tear that was created went unnoticed. However, if someone starts using the Tangle Thief again, there's going to be reports. The tears that it creates have the potential to create a vacuum effect."

"Do you mean they will start to pull things from this universe through the tear?" Julianna asked.

Cheng nodded, dropping his arm from around Knox's shoulders and using his hands as he explained. "Yes. Objects, people, and elements of the environment could be pulled through the tear. A great deal of radiation will also pour through from the other side, which will kill and destroy anything in the near vicinity."

Eddie whistled through his teeth. "That would stir up some attention."

"So we can safely say that, since there haven't been any reports like this, the Tangle Thief probably hasn't been used," Julianna guessed.

"See? Simple, like I said," Hatch yelled from his workstation.

"The details to help us apes understand the context would have assisted your point," Eddie called back.

Julianna stared at the case Hatch had thrust into her hands, before returning her gaze to Cheng. Knox, besides his black hair, obviously took after his mother in appearance. He was even taller than his father, especially when not slouching like he was now.

Hopefully once we locate and retrieve the Tangle Thief, that constant defeated demeanor will leave him.

"What's on the other side of the tear?" she asked.

Cheng scratched his chin. "It's only speculation," he said.

The scientist had practically returned to normal, based on Hatch's assessment. When they visited Onyx Station, he had been taken to a specialist for the damage he'd suffered when using the Tangle Thief. The results had been immediate, and now Cheng appeared more natural and less lost.

"Oh, we know that our speculations are usually correct," Hatch exclaimed, tinkering with a set of test tubes at his workstation—or at least making a show of not being interested in the current conversation.

"Right," Cheng said, letting out a breath. "We speculate, with a good deal of confidence, that on the other side of the tear would be a parallel universe."

"Far out!" Eddie yelled.

Julianna blinked. "Is that possible?"

Cheng shrugged. "It's the only thing that makes sense. The Tangle Thief operates using the principles from entanglement theory; to pull the object being taken, it would have to come through somewhere."

"So it's pulled through to the parallel universe and then popped back into ours in the location of the receiver?" Julianna asked.

Cheng tapped his fingers on his lips, musing on the question.

"Close enough!" Hatch yelled.

"Damn this stuff hurts my brain," Eddie said.

Cheng smiled. "That's perfectly normal. Richard Feynman said, 'If you think you understand quantum mechanics, you don't understand quantum mechanics.'"

"Who is he?" Eddie asked.

"He's a physicist who did a lot of work in the area of quantum electrodynamics," Cheng answered.

"You can thank him for nanotechnology and much of the technology that flies your ships," Hatch said.

For acting like he's irritated and not wanting to be part of the conversation, he sure has a lot to say today. Eddie pursed his lips in Julianna's direction. "Aren't you glad all we have to do is fly ships around and not wrap our heads around a science that no one understands?"

"I'm fairly certain that Dr. Feynman wouldn't have

wanted your job beating up bad guys," Cheng offered.

"Best job there is," Eddie said with a wink.

"Okay, back to the mission," Julianna said, steering the conversation onto the original track. "Knox, if we take you to Planet L2SCQ-6, do you think you can find where you hid the Tangle Thief?"

Knox nodded weakly.

Cheng slapped him gently on the back. "You'll definitely be able to find it, son. I knew you'd remember! You just needed some rest."

"You're welcome," Hatch yelled.

"Thanks...I think," Knox said.

Hatch looked up from his beaker, swirling a red liquid. "Oh, and you're unfired as soon as you return."

"What if I don't find the Tangle Thief?" Knox asked.

"Then you're fired again," Hatch said.

Eddie smiled broadly. "So no pressure."

"Don't worry," Cheng said to Knox. "We're going to find it."

"'We'?" Knox asked.

"Of course 'we'," Cheng said. "I'm going with you."

"It could be dangerous," Julianna warned.

"Then I'll face those dangers," Cheng fired back. "It's my fault that Dom—I mean, *Knox*, took the Tangle Thief."

"Jules, although Planet L2SCQ-6 is in the Frontier, I think the most trouble we'll run into is a few pirates who will immediately pee themselves when I draw a weapon," Eddie said, puffing out his chest.

"Planet L2SCQ-6 is full of pirates," Knox admitted.

"And we don't know what else," Julianna said. "I have a feeling that we should be prepared."

"Alright, then I'll tell Fletcher to have his team suit up," Eddie stated.

"Ricky Bobby, how long until we gate?" Julianna asked.

"Probably before you're done with your current conversation," Ricky Bobby answered.

"Damn, he's one efficient AI," Eddie said.

Is he inferring that I'm not? Pip asked, cutting into Julianna's thoughts.

You know that everything isn't always about you?

Isn't it?

"Let's roll out at 21:00." Julianna held up the case, looking at Hatch. "What's this for?"

"It's a case," Hatch said simply.

Eddie rolled his eyes, but smiled still. "I think he's intentionally trying to be unhelpful."

Hatch picked up a dropper and placed a single drop of liquid into the beaker in front of him. "I'm working on your leveling laser, actually. But if you're going to be that way, then I'll quit and work on the DeLorean."

"We were working on that together," Knox said quickly, his expression dropping with disappointment.

Hatch swiveled around to face him. "Does that mean you still want to be part of the project?"

"Yes, of course...I've been out of sorts," Knox explained.

Eddie offered him a sympathetic look. "Which is completely understandable."

"I believe he's *my* apprentice," Hatch said.

"So?" Eddied asked, looking confused.

Hatch lowered the beaker. "So stop babying him, or you'll undermine the discipline I've instilled."

"Being understanding isn't what I'd consider 'babying,'" Eddie argued.

"Last time I checked, no one asked you," Hatch said.

Knox stepped forward. "I want to work on the DeLorean with you...if I'm not fired, that is."

"Fine, we'll continue with the project when you return," Hatch said.

"And how is the leveling laser coming along?" Eddie asked.

Hatch's tentacles stretched to a workstation behind him, picking up another set of test tubes. "Taking over for Liesel posed some problems."

"Why is that?" Julianna asked.

"She isn't as meticulous as I am," Hatch answered.

"When do you think it will be complete?" Eddie asked.

"When it's done," Hatch said.

Eddie laughed. "Again, your brevity leaves me wanting more."

Julianna held up the case again. "What's in the case?"

Hatch sighed.

He appeared more bothered than usual. *Something is irking the mechanic. I'll ask him later, if he won't snap at me; well, even if he does.* She wasn't afraid of the grumpy Londil.

"Two sets of Saverus goggles," he answered.

"I don't expect that we'll need those for this mission," Eddie said.

Julianna unlatched the case, peering at the two sets of

goggles. "You never know, though. The Petigren were on Nexus."

"Yes, but their leads dried up there," Eddie reasoned. "They don't know to look on this Frontier planet."

Julianna closed the case. "I think underestimating the Saverus is a bad idea."

**Alpha-line Q-Ship, Outskirts Junkyard, Planet L2SCQ-6
in Frontier space**

Smoke billowed from the crumbling factories in the
distance. The entire planet was a series of grays. From the
sky, the entire surface appeared like one giant junkyard.

"Man, this place is a dump," Eddie said.

"Yeah," Knox agreed, his gaze searching the area as they
sped over the surface of the planet.

Eddie admonished himself. "Sorry, I know that you
spent a long time here. I'm sure there are many good things
about this planet."

Knox shook his head. "There's not."

Eddie scanned the gray landscape, trying to find an
open area to land. "Well, you don't have to worry about
that anymore. *Ricky Bobby* is your home now, and Ghost
Squadron is your family. That is, if you'll have us."

Knox looked over his shoulder at his father. There had
been some discussion of Cheng returning to the Federa-

tion to work directly for R&D. Eddie was certain that Knox felt torn between following his father and staying with Hatch and Ghost Squadron. The decision was his, though, and, as fond of the kid as Eddie had grown, he couldn't pressure him to stay. Hell, if given the choice, he'd always choose family over his career; he only wished he would have made that decision when he had the chance.

"Thanks," Knox said softly. Then he pointed. "The junkyard is over there."

"You mean the wasteland inside the wasteland?" Eddie lowered the ship, landing in a spot big enough for Julianna to fit alongside him with her Q-Ship.

"That's where I hid the Tangle Thief." Knox pointed in the direction of a severed ship. Only the stern of the large battlecruiser remained.

"Got it." Eddie pressed the button for his comm. "Carnivore, this is Black Beard. Do you read me?"

"Loud and clear," Lars said over the comm.

"What's your location?" Eddie asked.

"Entering the atmosphere now," Lars said.

Eddie stood, loading up his weapons. "Good. You and the Eagles keep an eye from the sky. We're heading out."

"Copy that," Lars said.

Eddie opened the rear hatch remotely, allowing Fletcher's team to disembark and spread out, sweeping the area.

The lieutenant was stationed on Julianna's ship, which was cloaked, same as theirs.

Eddie shot Knox an encouraging look. "You ready to do this?"

Knox gulped. "As ready as I'll ever be."

The smell of gasoline was strong in the air. Julianna stood at the back of the ship, looking at the junkyard in front of her. Fletcher was instructing his team outside.

I don't miss that smell.

I kind of like it.

You can smell?

Not technically.

Then, technically, how can you like the smell of a gas?

I've studied the characteristics of a large catalog of smells.

I could see that coming in handy if you're trying to help me investigate something.

This isn't always about you.

Touché.

Your French is beautiful.

Merci.

Gasoline reminds me a of a simpler time.

Simpler, true, but dirtier. It's currently polluting this planet's air.

Yes, I've already turned your respiratory intake down to minimize the amount of toxins you inhale.

Smart thinking.

I'd do the same for the captain, but, well...

Stop beating a dead horse.

That's such a strange expression.

We're going to discuss this integration business soon, so drop it.

When?

Soon.

I'm holding you to that.

I have no doubt about that. What's your obsession with being in Eddie's head, anyway?

Besides the fact that he said I could control his body?

Yes, aside from your damn obsession with control.

He's a man, if you haven't noticed.

I've noticed.

...Your body temperature just rose a degree.

No, it didn't, Julianna argued.

Anyway. My reason for wanting to be in Eddie's head is simple: I want the chance to hear, and be a part of, a man's thoughts—you know, since I'm a man and all.

You're male.

Same thing.

How do you think being in Eddie's head is going to be different than being in mine?

Men are simple.

I'm simple.

Pip laughed. **At any given moment, you're processing six to eight thoughts. As a female, your multitasking abilities are impressive, and also a bit overwhelming.**

So you want to be in Eddie's head so you can have some quiet time? Julianna laughed inwardly.

Should I tell the captain that you think his thoughts are akin to a tumbleweed rolling through the desert?

Don't put words in my mouth.

Fine. Yes, I'd like to study a simpler being. Understanding the difference between a man and a woman is a goal of mine. Call it a part of my dissertation.

Gender studies, huh?

When I'm done, you can call me 'Dr. Pip'.

Good thing I didn't name you Pepper, then.

I don't get the reference.

Go brush up on inferior Earth sodas.

Sure. I've got nothing else to do, Pip said as Julianna stepped out of the Q-Ship.

Fletcher's team dispersed, scanning the area as they marched through the wreckage.

Eddie smiled at her when she approached. "The greenish haze makes your eyes stand out," he said with a wink.

Julianna nodded to Knox and Cheng beside him. "The pollution is going to the captain's head. Take shallow breaths."

Cheng guffawed, but Knox ignored the interaction.

"I hid the Tangle Thief in there," the boy said, pointing at the severed stern of the battlecruiser. It was the largest thing in this area of the junkyard, being the size of a ten-story building.

Julianna started in the direction of the ship, intent on making this as fast a trip as possible.

"Carnivore, here," Lars said over the comm.

Julianna looked up, finding the Black Eagles streaking across the gray sky.

"This is Black Beard. Go on," Eddie answered.

"You have some company headed your way from the north end of the junkyard."

With his back against a rusted-out freight car, Fletcher lifted his rifle. He'd heard rustling from the other side of the car a moment before Lars's message broadcasted over the comm.

The sound was closer.

Not just closer, he thought. *Overhead.*

Drawing in a breath, Fletcher tore his gaze upward, but all he saw was the pile of old cars in front of him.

The sound came again, louder and right above him.

Whipping around, Fletcher aimed his rifle at the top of a freight car.

A Petigren cackled, its pointy teeth flashing bright against its dark face. The creature leapt off the top of the car, and Fletcher fired rapidly as he reversed out of the trajectory of the flying beast.

He shot the Petigren in the midsection several times. It landed on the ground in front of him with a *thud.*

Inhaling quickly, Fletcher looked up to find two more Petigrens, standing on top of the freight car.

Of course there would be fucking rats in the junkyard, he thought with a grimace.

"Want some cheese?" Fletcher asked, holding up his rifle, aiming it at the closest Petigren.

Its needle-like fingers were clenched by its chest, as it jerked its head to the side. The rat-man growled, narrowing his red eyes at Fletcher.

Fletcher was about to fire, when something caught his attention. He chanced a glance behind him; standing at the top of the pile of cars were two more Petigrens.

Fuck! Just when I thought this was going to be easy.

Spinning around, Fletcher fired at the Petigren on the surface of the freight car. He fell, and there were four more in its place.

Fucking rats! These things are multiplying.

Three jumped from above, and two others began climbing down the sides. Fletcher moved smoothly and swiftly to cover the avenues of approach, firing again and again, knocking out Petigrens with a single shot each. When they tumbled forward, their momentum threw off the balance of the stack of cars, and the top vehicle lurched forward.

Fucking hell.

The whole thing was about to topple.

Claws reached around Fletcher's neck from behind, and he threw his body weight forward, throwing the Petigren over his back. It squeaked when it landed.

The snarling of the other Petigrens racing for Fletcher was quickly drowned out by a cacophony of screeching metal, as the top car came free of the stack, turning end over end through the air. Two more immediately followed, gliding down behind the first.

Fletcher reached out, grabbing the closest approaching Petigren. He threw it hard in the opposite direction, and it slammed into the bottom of the stack before springing back to its feet. As the Petigren readied to come at Fletcher again, the first falling car landed on top of it, smashing it flat with a *squish*.

"If the Petigrens are here, that means the Saverus are, too," Julianna stated after getting Lars's report.

Eddie disappeared to the Q-Ship and returned a moment later, carrying the Saverus goggles. He handed one set to Julianna and the other to Knox.

"We're going to have to share, but we should pull these up every time we encounter anyone."

All of the color had drained from Cheng's face. Encountering the alien race who had imprisoned him for almost a decade wasn't easy.

Knox, seeing his father's palpable fear, said, "Dad, you don't have to go with me."

Cheng shook his head. "Of course I do."

"No, you don't," Knox argued. "Stay in the Q-Ship. It's secure, and you'll be safe there."

"What about you, though?" Cheng asked.

"I have to go," Knox said.

"You don't, actually," Julianna countered. "Tell us where the Tangle Thief is located, and we'll retrieve it."

Knox was shaking his head before she was done speaking. "I've got to do this. I'm the reason it went missing. I need to be the one who finds it."

"Neither of you are trained for combat," Eddie interjected. "It could be dangerous out there. The Petigrens are vicious, and the Saverus... well, they're fucking snakes."

"Knox, they're right," Cheng said to his son.

Knox ran his top teeth over bottom lip several times. "I grew up on this planet. I may not know how to fight, but I know how to stay alive. I'm going."

"Yeah, fine," Eddie stated.

"Cheng, I think you should stay in the Q-Ship," Julianna said.

The scientist gave her a look of alarm. "If Knox is going, then I am, too."

"The captain and I will have our work cut out for us protecting him," Julianna explained. "You don't *need* to go; if the Saverus get ahold of you again, they'll take you prisoner, use you for leverage against us. That's not something we should risk."

Cheng looked between Julianna and Knox. He swallowed. "I haven't been around to protect Knox for so long. He needs to recover the device, and I need to be there to help if I can. I won't get in the way, I promise."

Julianna nodded. She wasn't going to argue anymore; they were wasting time. "Okay, stick together people."

Verdok stood in his natural form, between the wreckage of a tank and a pile of farming equipment. This planet mostly appeared to be the trashcan of the system. He'd been staked out for a few days and had watched shuttles fly in and dump loads of junk and garbage.

Whoever was flying the ships didn't care about this planet, or the fact that the offloaded trash would contaminate the water supply. They didn't concern themselves with the race who called the unclassified planet home, either. The natives had probably been overrun long ago; maybe they were even extinct, deprived as they were of a clean supply of water. Or maybe, like the

Saverus, they were biding their time, preparing to strike back.

Verdok slipped into the shadows. "The boy is here and will lead them to the Tangle Thief," he said to the three other Saverus.

"Our patience has paid off," one of them said.

"Yes. The Petigrens will serve as a distraction, overwhelming their other forces, while we track the boy and his friends to the device," Verdok explained. He shifted into the form of the woman holding a rifle, having catalogued her identity when in Area 126.

"One of you change to the form of Cheng, the scientist we had imprisoned, since we know he's here," Verdok ordered.

The closest Saverus shifted until he had taken on the appearance of the scientist who had never given them any helpful information regarding the Tangle Thief.

"You two, take on any human form you wish; once you've gotten close to a member of Ghost Squadron, steal their identity," Verdok said.

The Saverus shifted into different forms, one male and the other female.

"We must stay back until they lead us to the Tangle Thief," Verdok ordered. "Once we find out exactly where it is, then we can do what we do best."

The Saverus in the form of Cheng smiled disingenuously. "Confuse and deceive."

21

Black Eagle, Outskirts Junkyard, Planet L2SCQ-6 in Frontier space

It astounded Lars, how large the junkyard was. It covered at least four square miles. But more staggering than its physical size was the sizable infestation of Petigrens.

He'd first noticed the rat-men, crawling among the wreckage of an ancient plane, as he circled the perimeter of the junkyard. Now that he was on alert for them, he noted that there had to be a few hundred. The Saverus had been expecting them, and came prepared for a fight.

But the Petigrens couldn't touch Lars in the Black Eagle.

He'd flown over the same section twice, ensuring that only Petigrens littered the area. The rat-men scurried around the heaps of junk as if they were hunting for food.

Soon they'd realize that Ghost Squadron was there;

Lars had to decrease their numbers before that happened. Otherwise the ground forces would be overwhelmed.

Lars locked his sights on a pack of Petigrens clogging a path. He never enjoyed killing, but in taking out these evil creatures, he felt like he'd been sent to clean out an infestation. Lars pulled the trigger, unleashing a barrage of bullets.

"Exterminate. Exterminate," he said, watching as the Petigrens were ripped apart by the rapid fire.

Petigrens shot out of various hiding places, scared by the sudden noise. Lars swerved the Black Eagle around, taking aim at another swarm. He was about to celebrate an early victory when a ship dropped out of the low clouds overhead.

Lars's chest tightened at the sight of the chrome ship. *Dammit, not again.*

Nona had pulled herself into the top of the old fire tower when Lars's voice crackled over the comm.

"Enemy ships have appeared," the Kezzin said.

"Dammit!" Eddie yelled over the comm. "The shapeshifting ones?"

"Yes, sir," Lars said.

"Avoid any air attacks," Eddie ordered. "Focus all efforts on defending the ground forces. Do not, I repeat, do *not* fire at aircraft. They're trying to confuse us, and we can't risk shooting down one of our own."

"Copy that, Black Beard," Lars said.

Nona looked up from the edge of the tower. In the gray sky filled with ominous clouds, she counted half a dozen Black Eagles. A moment later, the chrome ships materialized, and she realized that they'd been there all along, blending in with the sky due to their mirrored appearance.

She pressed her scope to her eye and looked up at the sky, finding one of the Saverus's ships. The chrome vehicle flashed, sending out a blinding light, and was replaced by a Black Eagle.

Whoa.

She'd heard that the Saverus's ships could shapeshift, but seeing it firsthand was trippy. Nona had always been happy with her choice to become a sniper, but sometimes she'd wondered if she'd do well as a pilot. For once, she was wholeheartedly glad that she didn't take that path. The pilots overhead had gone from having an easy job of picking off Petigrens from the safety of their ship, to being surrounded by a disguised enemy.

Nona swiveled her rifle down, scanning the area for Petigrens. She was definitely in the safest place for this battle, with a bird's eye view of the junkyard, and no enemy who could easily touch her. She stabilized her rifle on the balustrade of the tower, ensuring she had the most stable platform she could get.

A Petigren scurried from behind a pile of old, beaten up appliances.

Time to start picking off rats.

Nona rested her cheek on her rifle, looking straight through the scope and finding her target. She focused on the reticle, set up her sight alignment, and released the safety, conscious of the loud click the action made. Placing the pad of her finger on the trigger, she started the steady build of pressure until the rifle fired.

The bullet struck the Petigren in the back of the head. One shot. One kill.

Julianna was at the front of the retrieval team, while Eddie brought up the rear. The putrid smell of rot mixed with dust wafted through the metal structures all around them. If Eddie had a chance, he'd pause to appreciate the different piles of junk they passed. In a strange way, they were beautiful, these unwanted items piled together, accidentally making sculptures, works of art.

Julianna halted. Her back tensed. She slid her gaze to meet Eddie's, and with a slight hand gesture, motioned to something on the other side of a bus that lay nearly on its side. It was barely being held up by the scrap pieces of cars stacked under it.

Eddie nodded, acknowledging Julianna's signal, and released the safety on his rifle.

Then he motioned for Knox and Cheng to move back. His enhanced hearing picked up on the scratching seconds before a Petigren leapt out from behind the bus.

Julianna shot it twice and threw a glance at Eddie. "Fucker never stood a chance," she said, glowing from the adrenaline rush.

"Damn straight," Eddie replied, catching sight of

another approaching Petigren in his peripheral. "This one is mine."

He took a step forward, raising his rifle.

A Petigren with zero sense of self-preservation ran straight for them.

Aiming, Eddie took a breath, holding it as he pulled the trigger. The Petigren fell on his hairy face, his feet tumbling over his head from the momentum.

"They really are dumb little shits," Julianna spat, assessing the path. It was clear ahead.

"Guys?" Knox's tone was apprehensive.

Eddie turned to find exactly why. Behind them, scurrying over broken cars and around mountains of junk, were dozens of Petigrens. With their teeth bared and eyes glowing red, the beasts looked hungry.

"Fucking hell!" Eddie yelled.

"Get moving," Julianna ordered, urging Knox and Cheng into the lead and pushing them down the clear path.

Eddie unleashed a volley of fire, taking down a few of the Petigrens. For every one he hit, though, three more took its place. He sprinted after the group as he reloaded, fully aware that the Petigrens were closing in on them. *The little shits are fast as hell.* Eddie and Julianna could have outrun them, but Knox and Cheng would have been left behind.

After going through another magazine, Eddie threw his rifle over his shoulder. He pulled his pistols from his holsters and held up both guns, alternating shots, taking out Petigrens one at a time.

"Eddie!" Julianna yelled behind him.

"What?" he asked, not daring to turn around.

"We're boxed in!" she exclaimed.

Julianna stepped up beside him, taking over the coverage. He spun around to find that they were in a dead-end of a valley of junk. It had all been pushed up into slanted walls, and the Petigrens were closing in from every angle.

"Fuck!" Eddie yelled. "We're going to have to reroute."

"Knox says that the Tangle Thief is that way!" Julianna said, motioning in the distance before firing beside Eddie. They were barely keeping the Petigrens back.

"Hey, Knox!" Eddie called, throwing a glance at his back.

Knox stood beside his father, looking for a way through the junk. "Yeah!" he replied over the gunfire.

"See that bulldozer?" Eddie motioned to the far left, where a faded yellow bulldozer blended in with the junk surrounding it.

"Yeah!"

"If we cover you, do you think you can get to it and clear a path?" Eddie fired around the bulldozer, which was only fifteen yards away.

Knox didn't answer, but he sprinted for the vehicle.

"Good call!" Julianna said.

"Let's hope it works," Eddie said, reloading.

Knox hoped that operating a bulldozer was similar to flying a ship. He sprinted for the equipment, zigzagging on the path to avoid rogue Petigrens. Eddie and Julianna were providing coverage, but they all knew their ammo wouldn't last for long, being boxed in like that.

Knox climbed into the bulldozer, which wasn't easy; the giant machine was the size of a small house. It had obviously been what created the wall of junk around them, though.

If it can make a wall of debris, then it can tear one down, Knox thought.

His instincts took over as soon as he slid into the seat, and the bulldozer fired up with a loud roar.

The Petigrens changed their attack, running on all fours in his direction.

An abrupt laugh fell from Knox's mouth. Eddie wanted him to clear a path so they could escape the Petigrens, but maybe Knox could clear the rats instead.

The bulldozer lurched forward when Knox released the brake. The machine was surprisingly fast, speeding in the direction of a pack of Petigrens, who ran straight for the blade. Knox shoveled them aside like trash. The ones who continued speeding toward the bulldozer were caught under the track and run over, making for a bumpy ride. Knox grimaced slightly at the crunching and banging as he cleared a path through the bodies.

The approaching rats peeled back, changing course after watching the destruction the bulldozer was capable of. Knox turned the machine, heading for the wall of junk. He slid the blade under the bottom of the wall.

The bulldozer hesitated for a moment before pushing boldly forward. Knox plunged through the wreckage creating a path to the other side. He could see the battlecruiser clearly. The place where he'd hidden the Tangle Thief.

Knox's excitement doubled when he broke through the wall to find a clear path leading directly to the battlecruiser.

Pulling the bulldozer to the side, Knox turned it off and hopped down from the seat.

A Petigren screamed from the top of the machine, and Knox whipped around, his eyes wide. Three Petigrens were perched on its roof.

Knox reached for a long pole protruding from a stack of rubbish, brandishing the makeshift weapon.

The beasts leapt off the bulldozer, landing on their feet. Their claws reached for Knox, scratching through the air.

Swinging the pole around, Knox knocked one in the head, but another caught him around the shoulder.

"Hey!" Knox yelled, wondering where the group was. Gunfire echoed from around the corner where they'd been stationed.

Knox ducked as another Petigren tried to grab for him. He brought the pole down on the rat-man's head, but it wasn't much of a deterrent. Yet another one caught him around the neck, biting him hard.

He screamed, whirling around, trying to free himself of the Petigren. He threw his back into a car, pinning the rat to it. It growled, scratching at Knox's face.

Julianna and Eddie sprinted around the corner with Cheng behind them.

Two more Petigrens leapt around the bulldozer, headed straight for Knox. He threw himself back once more, crushing the Petigren on his back against the car, then he dropped his weight, pulling the beast over his head and down to the ground.

Julianna roundhouse kicked one of the Petigrens, and Eddie punched another in the face. Knox spun around, checking the path ahead. It was clear. For now.

When he turned back, Eddie and Julianna had made quick work of the beasts surrounding them.

"Dad! Come on!" Knox yelled to his father, who was standing idly several yards away. His eyes were pointed up, and apprehension was heavy in his gaze.

Bringing Cheng was definitely a mistake. It's too soon to put him in a situation of this sort.

"Come on, Cheng!" Eddie encouraged when he hadn't moved.

Petigrens sprang off the top of the wall of junk, landing in front of the scientist. Startled, he jumped back several feet.

"Dad!" Knox yelled.

"I've got this!" Eddie said, holding up a hand to stop Knox before he could spring after his father. The captain sprinted for the Petigrens as Cheng ran from them.

22

Black Eagle, Outskirts Junkyard, Planet L2SCQ-6 in Frontier space

Lars sped the Black Eagle along the perimeter of the junkyard. He'd caught sight of a row of parked shuttles in the same chrome finish as the single flyers.

This must be how the Saverus transported so many Petigrens to the junkyard. It's also probably their way home.

"I think these guys deserve to be stranded on this trash planet," Lars said, releasing a missile. It raced over the junkyard, exploding a shuttle upon impact.

"Yahoo!" Lars yelled victoriously.

"Carnivore, what's got you so excited?" Lone Wolf asked over the comm.

"Found their transport ships. I'm adding them to the junkyard," Lars said.

"Oh, then I guess that's not you racing in my direction," Lone Wolf said.

"Not me, Lone Wolf," Lars replied.

"This is Escrema. That isn't me, either," she said.

"Fuck!" Lone Wolf yelled. "Which would explain why that traitor Black Eagle started firing at me."

"Get out of there," Lars ordered, firing another missile.

If he thought he'd be able to easily pick off the transport ships, he was wrong. He'd caught the attention of three Black Eagles, which were now racing in his direction.

"I'm guessing you all aren't coming to assist me on the perimeter?" Lars asked.

"Nope," Escrema answered.

"Trapeze here. I'm not even close to that vicinity."

"Not me! I'm trying to give this imposter the slip," Lone Wolf groaned.

The approaching Black Eagles flew in formation, making quick progress toward Lars. He had been ordered not to fire on the Black Eagles, which meant that he had to outfly these Saverus to survive.

At first, Nona was able to casually pick off Petigrens as they filtered onto the path below. Quickly, though, she had more targets than she could easily take down.

Where did all of these fuckers come from?

"Fuller, what's your position?" Fletcher asked over the comm.

"Firetower in central area," Nona answered, taking down another Petigren.

The ones around her target scampered away in fear,

many of them searching over their shoulder for the shooter.

"I was afraid of that. Your position is compromised," Fletcher said.

Nona straightened, leaning over the railing of the fire tower. Three Petigrens were crawling up the side of the structure.

"Shit," Nona breathed, pulling her pistol from her holster.

"I'm not far from your location," Fletcher told her. "I'll try and get over there to help."

"Thanks." Nona fired, shooting down the closest Petigren.

The gunfire attracted the attention of many of the rats swarming on the ground. They raced in Nona's direction as if they were magnetized.

"Make it fast," Nona said. "It would appear that I've summoned the zombies."

Julianna read the hesitation in Knox's eyes as Eddie ran after Cheng. He wanted to go after his father, but he had another job, and they both knew it.

"He'll be okay," Julianna said, tilting Knox's head to the side and gauging the wound in his neck.

He gasped in pain, but stifled it quickly. The bite mark was deep and bleeding quite a bit. Julianna pulled her bandana from her pocket and stuffed it into Knox's hand.

"Apply pressure," she ordered, scanning the path ahead

before marching forward.

"What are you doing?" Knox asked, not having moved.

"We've got a job to finish." Julianna pointed with her rifle in the direction of the broken-down battlecruiser.

"But my dad…" Knox turned to the path that was now empty, the Petigrens having followed Cheng the other direction.

"Black Beard, do you copy?" Julianna asked into the comm.

There was no answer.

"This is Strong Arm," Julianna tried again. "Black Beard, are you there?"

Dammit, comms are down.

Is that your way of asking for my help?

What do you think?

I think we need to work on your people skills.

Julianna shook her head, meeting Knox's gaze. "Don't worry. Eddie will protect him," she assured him, trying to inject conviction into her voice.

The truth was that, although she believed in Eddie, she had her doubts if anyone was safe in this maze of junk, with rabid rat-men on the loose. They had struggled to hold the Petigrens back earlier and were almost overrun. If they were attacked like that again, she didn't have enough ammo to take them all down.

Knox pressed the rag to his wound and glanced over his shoulder one last time.

"Lead the way," Julianna urged him forward gently—for her. "The sooner we get what we came here for, the sooner we can get out of here."

He nodded slowly, joining her on the path.

Cheng hadn't taken a moment to think. Only reacted. And now the Petigrens were on his heels, closing in on him. His chest ached as he pushed to run faster. Something ripped at his shirt, trying to get a hold of him. A Petigren leapt, catching him around the ankle, and pulled him to the ground.

Cheng fell, biting on dirt. Dust filled his lungs. A Petigren jumped onto his back when he pushed up to all fours, and its weight dragged him back to the ground. He tried to roll over, but he was too weak to fight the monster.

Suddenly the Petigren was gone. Cheng rolled over, blinking at the person before him. Julianna was holding the Petigren in the air. She slammed her knee into its chest before throwing it to the ground, and the nearby pack of Petigrens paused, making a greedy cackling sound as they hunched low. Julianna aimed her weapon at the rats, her eyes narrowed.

"Get out of here!" Julianna yelled.

To Cheng's surprise, the Petigrens whipped around, racing on all fours down a side path.

Dusting off her arm, Julianna looked at Cheng. "Are you alright?"

Cheng glanced in the direction he'd come from. *How did she get to me?* He hadn't seen her pursuing them.

"Come on, we've got to get out of here." Julianna extended a hand to Cheng.

He didn't take it, pushing up from the ground on his own. "How did you get over here?"

Julianna smiled wide, something he'd never seen her do. "I took a shortcut when those animals raced after you. I think we're safe for now, but we need to get to our ship."

"Why do we need to do that?" Cheng asked, his adrenaline beating in his head like a drum.

"We're being overwhelmed," Julianna stated, turning around and scanning the area behind them. "The ship is cloaked, and I'm all turned around. Do you remember where we left it?"

Pip would know exactly where the Q-Ship is parked, therefore Julianna would, too. Cheng took a step back. He was unarmed and had to play this right.

"Where are Knox and Eddie?" Cheng asked.

"They went to retrieve the Tangle Thief," Julianna answered. "We're going to get the ship and pick them up."

This Saverus was going to take the Q-Ship and leave the others stranded. Cheng couldn't allow that to happen. He knew little about the Saverus, even after being imprisoned by them for almost ten years; however, he did know that it was best to play along and leave them with the illusion that they were still in control.

"The ship is this way." Cheng pointed in the direction where he'd come from.

Julianna squinted. "How is that possible?"

"We have to cut around this section and then double back, don't you remember?"

The imposter nodded. "Yeah, of course I do. You take the lead."

Cheng swallowed hard and started off, holding onto hope that he was leading the Saverus back toward the others.

Eddie zigzagged through the intersecting paths. Petigrens jumped out from behind old refrigerators and other appliances, and he picked off each one as efficiently as he could.

Everything had happened so fast. Cheng, overcome by fear, had moved so quickly that Eddie had lost him.

A pack of Petigrens crowded a path that Eddie was about to bypass. He doubled back; where there were rats, there was bait. Eddie fired until he was empty, and thankfully that's all it took to take down the pack.

Eddie leapt over their fallen bodies and paused, having heard a voice.

"I'm pretty sure we're getting close," Cheng said, seeming to be yelling.

Who is he talking to? Did he join up with someone from Fletcher's team? Eddie wondered.

Sliding up to a wall of junk, Eddie reloaded. He only had another couple of rounds left. They'd gone through them so fast, not having expected it possible to meet so many Petigrens. The sound of gunfire could be heard all around in the junkyard. Eddie hoped that the others weren't close to running out of ammo, too.

The footsteps were getting closer. Eddie braced himself.

"I think it's down here!" Cheng exclaimed, which was strange.

Unless...

Cheng came around the corner, Julianna at his back. The scientist's eyes widened when he saw Eddie. He dove to the side in a blur. "It's not Julianna. Shoot it!"

Julianna stepped around the corner, holding a rifle at the ready. Eddie didn't have to pull up the Saverus goggles to know that the person before him wasn't Julianna. She whipped her rifle around and pointed it straight at him, menace in her gaze like he'd never seen before.

Eddie shot the imposter once in the chest, knocking her to the ground.

He sucked in a breath, sudden doubt overwhelming him. *What if I was wrong? What if Cheng was wrong?*

The scientist was at his side now. "She asked me to take her to the Q-Ship."

Eddie stepped forward, his eyes wide at the sight of Julianna sprawled on the ground and bleeding. "What?" Eddie asked. "*That's* why you thought it wasn't Julianna?"

"It *isn't* Julianna," Cheng insisted, but panic was written on his face as he looked between the body and Eddie.

"Then why hasn't it shifted back?" Eddied darted forward.

"What?" Cheng asked.

"Saverus shift back to their natural form when unconscious!" Eddie yelled. *I shot Julianna! Will her nanocytes save her from a bullet wound to the chest?*

Crouched by her side, he reached out and checked her pulse. It was weak, but there.

Her eyes fluttered open.

"Jules, is that you?" Eddie asked, desperation in his voice.

"Yes, and you murdered me," she said through ragged breaths.

"No!" Eddie screamed, lifting Julianna into his arms, cradling her bleeding body against his.

She choked on a cough, blood sputtering from her mouth. Then she fell completely still.

I'm cursed. Utterly cursed. This time he hadn't failed to save someone he loved—he'd killed her himself.

"Captain," Cheng dared to say, placing a hand on Eddie's shoulder.

Eddie shook his head, eyes pressed tightly closed.

"Captain, I think you should see this," Cheng said, now shaking his shoulder.

"What?!" Eddie yelled, his eyes bolting open. He stumbled back, dropping the snake he'd been holding. "I-I-It wasn't her," he stuttered, pointing at the iridescent blue snake that was the size of a large man.

"I told you it was a Saverus," Cheng said.

"But when I asked, it said...I'd murdered her," Eddie stammered, his mind and chest cramping.

With bitterness in his eyes, Cheng said, "They deceive. That's what they do. Even with their last breath."

The battlecruiser looked to have been sawed in half, leaving the mid-section wide open to the junkyard. Each deck was exposed, and wires and debris hung from the severed floors. It was strange. It reminded her of Harley, how he'd looked with his stomach split open and his guts hanging out.

"What happened to this ship?" Julianna asked, mostly to herself.

"I don't know," Knox said. "In its day, though, it would have been incredible."

"Let's hope that *Ricky Bobby* never experiences a similar fate."

Knox nodded. "The Tangle Thief is on the fifth level."

"You really did go to quite the extremes to hide it, didn't you?"

"It may sound crazy, but I knew that one day someone would be searching for it."

"That doesn't sound as crazy as you think."

Julianna stared up at the ship, realizing that getting into it would be a feat, and dangerous as hell.

"Then hopefully you won't think it's strange that I knew it would be Ghost Squadron looking for the device," Knox said quietly.

"How could you possibly know that?" Julianna asked.

Knox gulped, his gaze stretching across the junkyard before he turned back to the battlecruiser. "When I was in Area 126 as a child, the hologram, Kyra, said that one day someone would come looking for the Tangle Thief— someone who knew me. She called them my 'team.'"

"She was referring to us?" Julianna asked, perplexed.

Knox nodded. "I think so."

"Your memory is back? You're able to recall everything

from that time?"

"Yes, and it's getting clearer now that we are here. I think using the Tangle Thief blocked it all out, but whatever Dr. Harrison did has helped to unlock it," Knox said.

Julianna massaged her temples, trying to make sense of this all. "How could Kyra know that we would come looking for the Tangle Thief in the future?"

"Time isn't linear for her," Knox shrugged.

He's exactly right, Pip said.

That doesn't make sense.

It does if you understand that the space-time continuum works differently for various beings. For Kyra, there is no past or future; there's only a series of 'now' moments.

That doesn't make sense.

You're repeating yourself.

Julianna huffed her frustration.

Knox pointed to the side of the battlecruiser. "The easiest way up is climbing along the side."

"There are no stairs?" Julianna asked.

"Not that I found, and I searched pretty extensively," Knox said.

"Did you live here?"

With a haunted expression in his eyes, Knox nodded. "I think so. For a little while, at least. Until Mateo found me."

A small shiver ran down Julianna's spine. She couldn't imagine being a child living in a junkyard on an unclassified planet. The fact that Knox became anything was impressive. *Or* maybe it was because of the hardships he endured.

23

Outskirts Junkyard, Planet L2SCQ-6 in Frontier space

The fire tower was crawling with Petigrens. As fast as Nona was at shooting them down, she couldn't get to every side quick enough.

Fletcher had some luck with clearing the north-facing side, but he was too far away to be much more help. He spotted a Petigren as it climbed over the banister, having made it to the top of the tower. Nona's back was to it as she was focused on another one that was only a few feet from her.

"Fuller, you have a trespasser," Fletcher said into the comm.

No answer.

He tapped the comm in his ear, trying to reset it, and a high-pitched noise sounded in his head. He pulled the comm out, wincing from the assault to this eardrum.

Dammit, the comms are out again. This happened the last time the Saverus invaded... It must be a tactic. Fletcher had to hope that Pip found a fix, otherwise rounding up his team was going to be difficult.

The Petigren Fletcher had seen caught Nona off-guard and grabbed her around the neck from behind. Another made it to the top, and was spilling over the side. Fletcher ran for the firetower. *There's no way I'm letting the best member of my team be taken down by fucking rat-men.*

Knox grunted, pulling himself up to the third deck. Julianna peered down from the fifth level, her hands on her hips.

"Try using your legs for leverage. It will help," Julianna offered.

"Being enhanced would also help," Knox said, his face pinched red.

Julianna had made scaling the battlecruiser look easy. She'd offered to go behind Knox and give him a boost up at each floor, but he'd refused.

A hallway, severed in half, stretched out in front of Julianna. Wires trailed overhead and spilled out of the frayed edge where she stood. She guessed this was a rooming corridor, based on the layout. A buzzing noise echoed from deep inside the ship.

The ship is still alive, Pip observed, sounding impressed.

That doesn't make any sense.

Are you intentionally trying to get on my nerves?

Maybe.

Well, it actually does make sense and it's entirely possible.

Where is the ship getting its power from?

Magic.

Come on now, Julianna urged, watching Knox's slow progress.

You know damn well how the Etheric works.

Is there anyone left on this ship? An entity of any sort?

I don't think so. I was able to access the mainframe and learned that this ship was decommissioned.

Because it was cut into pieces?

Actually it was decommissioned and then cut into pieces, which were then scattered in different disposal areas.

And now, the question you're waiting for: why?

I think it suffered from a virus of sorts. But I'm still trying to crack the encryption on the protected files.

Well, my curiosity is definitely piqued. The ship doesn't look old enough to be decommissioned.

It isn't. It's in really good condition... but I sense there's a fatal flaw.

Not exactly what I wanted to hear before a journey into the belly of it.

You'll be okay. Or you won't.

Thanks for the sympathy.

In other news, comms will be back online in thirty-seven seconds.

Could you be a bit more specific with the ETA?

Ha. Ha.

Knox's red face peeked over the side of the floor as he

heaved himself up, and Julianna reached down and pulled him all the way over. He rolled onto his back, breathing hard.

"You made that trip every time you came here?" Julianna asked, an eyebrow raised in surprise.

Knox shook his head. "I only came up here once. I lived on the lowest deck."

"Good call. When you've caught your breath, let's set off. Comms will be back online soon."

Knox nodded, drawing a large breath.

Julianna looked out over the junkyard. From her high vantage point, she could see the sheer number of Petigrens they were facing. The creatures congested many areas in the junkyard; in the center of the expansive lot, Petigrens were even crawling up the side of an old fire tower.

If Ghost Squadron stayed any longer, they would definitely be overrun.

———

"Black Beard, do you read me?" Julianna said over the comm.

Eddie had never been so happy to hear her voice. For the rest of his life, he would be haunted by the vision of shooting her in the chest.

"Strong Arm," Eddie said. "Comms are back?"

"Pip took his sweet damn time," she replied.

Eddie smiled. "Are you alright?"

"Yes, Knox and I are on the fifth level of the battlecruiser," Julianna answered.

Eddie shot a hopeful look at Cheng, who looked extremely concerned. "Great. We're headed that way."

"Cheng is alright, then?" Julianna asked.

"Yes, tell Knox that he's fine and he even took out a Saverus," Eddie said, giving the credit to Cheng because he did in fact deserve it. The scientist had spotted the Saverus for what it was, without the goggles.

"Good news. Okay, we're headed into the ship."

Julianna sounded antsy.

"We'll meet you there. Out."

Knox's face lit up with relief when hearing that Cheng was all right.

"Lead the way," Julianna said after a moment, getting his attention back to the task at hand. She extended her arm to the broken hallway.

Knox started forward, walking close to the wall since the remaining hallway was only about two feet wide. They were halfway to the next intersecting corridor when his foot broke through the floor, and he fell through up to his knee. Julianna leapt forward, grabbed him by the arm, and yanked him upwards.

"Be careful," she warned. "This ship is fraying."

Knox nodded, staying closer to the wall as he cleared the last section. It was like walking on the edge of a building.

At the next hallway, Julianna was accosted by the smell of roasted chicken, wafting through the air. Suddenly she had the urge to pull off her boots and splash in water. Julianna was shocked when she giggled at the thought of sneaking into the kitchen and stealing a cookie.

She covered her mouth and looked at Knox, but he was laughing, too.

"Isn't it a great place?" Knox asked.

"What?" Julianna asked. "What are you experiencing?"

"Good emotions. Memories. Things that make me feel better," Knox told her.

Not better, Pip cut in.

Have you figured out what the ship's virus does?

Julianna was having great difficulty working out the strange emotions flowing through her. Knox was right. Something was making her feel happier.

Yes. The ship isn't trying to make you feel better; it's trying to make you stay. Like a drug that keeps calling you back to it.

What?

The virus pulls memories from your cortex and supplies the details to you, putting you in a state of euphoria.

They decommissioned a ship for that? That's bizarre. Some people would pay extra for that experience. Julianna giggled, unable to control herself.

Not if they knew the intention behind it. The euphoria a host feels is only a distraction.

From what? What is it really doing?

It's absorbing the inhabitants of the ship, literally robbing them of their life force. But they don't notice it

because of the good feelings. By the time they realize something is wrong, it's too late.

Julianna's mouth dropped open. *That's where the power is coming from?*

Bingo. This ship is alive because it's feasted on so many people and absorbed their consciousness.

Wow. How many people did this ship absorb?

Three crews consisting of over a thousand members. That was before they figured out what was going on.

So it's a vampire ship. It distracts you and then sucks you dry.

Not you, though. Again, you owe me big.

The strange euphoria fell away, and Julianna felt back to normal, which she wasn't sure was a good thing. Being on cloud nine was really nice.

Did you find a way to block the virus?

Of course, because I'm amazing.

Or was it my nano?

Pip sighed. **Well, they might have kicked in and protected you from the virus, but I'm taking credit.**

So Eddie will be all right?

The captain will be fine, but you're going to have to be quick getting Knox in and out of here.

He left on his own before, though.

It was easier to escape because the ship is in pieces, and the outside world is right there. But could you imagine being deep in space, locked inside this ship?

Wow.

So escaping the ship wasn't a problem, and it still

shouldn't be; the longer that Knox is in here, though, the more life force the ship will leech from him.

Is that part of how he lost his memory? Julianna mused.

Quite possibly. It appears that the virus needs a solid three days to steal a person's life completely, but it is still doing its damage in the meantime.

Julianna shivered at the thought, then turned to Knox. "It's go time. Where's the Tangle Thief?"

The smile that formed lit up Knox's face, making his eyes sparkle. "This way," he sang, skipping down the corridor.

Lars rolled his ship, narrowly escaping a barrage from a Saverus's Black Eagle. He wasn't sure how much longer they could keep this up. The pilots weren't having much luck with attacking the Petigrens because the Saverus ships were constantly on their asses.

"Black Beard? This is Carnivore," Lars said over the comm, grateful to again be connected to the ground forces.

"Carnivore, go ahead," Eddie replied.

"Our defense efforts are being completely squashed. We can't help with the Petigrens because we're overrun by these Saverus ships."

Lars didn't like that his every word sounded like a complaint, but it was the truth. They'd been flying around, doing their best to avoid the Saverus, with no time for anything else. Their efforts felt counterproductive at this point.

"The ground forces are experiencing the same overrun," Fletcher chimed in, to Lars's relief. "We were nearly taken out at the fire tower. We've had to back down from our offensive tactics and retreat."

"Carnivore, can you make another sweep? Provide a round of cover for the ground forces?" Eddie asked.

"Absolutely," Lars confirmed. "We'll do whatever we can to get them out of there safely."

A loud sigh echoed over the fleet comm. "Black Eagles, this is your captain. Make one last sweep, starting at the northern border and moving south. I want you to draw as many Petigrens away from our Q-Ship locations as possible," Eddie ordered. "Once the ground forces have made it to the ship, retreat."

Knox appeared to be led by an innate force. He still let out a small chuckle every now and then, but once Julianna explained to him what the virus did, he was much more in control. Knowledge was indeed power.

"It's down here." He pointed at a hallway at the far end of the rooming corridor.

They were at the stern, but the greenish light from outside could be seen down the hallway. Julianna felt better as long as she could see the junkyard; it let her know that they weren't going to be stuck in this vampiric ship.

"Where is it?" Julianna asked.

"I hid it under a loose panel in the floor," Knox said.

Julianna was impressed. "Damn, no one was going to accidentally stumble across that."

"I told you," Knox said, laughing loudly.

It was such an uncharacteristic thing for him to do, that it brought home the fact that the laughter was only distracting him from his life force being drained.

"There you are!" Eddie yelled from the far side of the corridor, where they'd come from.

"Hey!" Julianna yelled, strangely relieved to see him. "Where's Cheng?"

Eddie indicated with his head. "He's coming."

"Maybe it's better if he doesn't come all the way up here; there's something wrong with the ship," Julianna explained.

"Besides the fact that it has been sawed into pieces?"

Eddie laughed at his joke, but not just once. His laughter filled the air like he'd been infected with it.

Knox joined him, doubling over in laughter.

I thought you said the virus wouldn't affect us, Julianna asked Pip.

You were vulnerable for about ten seconds before your nano kicked in.

Eddie was still laughing, although Knox seemed to have regained control.

Julianna pulled the Saverus goggles up from where they'd been hanging around her neck. She turned the lens once, and the image of Eddie disappeared, replaced by that of a giant, purple snake.

"Fucker!" Julianna yelled, releasing the goggles. She pointed her rifle, but the Saverus figured out he'd been caught. Still in Eddie's form, he darted back the way he'd come. Julianna took off after him, yelling to Knox as she sprinted, "Get it and get out of here!"

Once at the side of the ship, the Saverus shifted into its natural form and slithered down, making quick progress to the ground. From the fifth level, she spotted Eddie—the real one—and Cheng, peeling around a pile of junk.

"There!" Julianna pointed at the snake, which was now on the ground. It resumed the form of Eddie and darted around the battlecruiser.

"Got him!" Eddie called back to her.

Julianna was about to rush back to help Knox when something caught her attention: partially obstructed from view, crouched down behind a car, was a figure she didn't recognize. Cheng dashed by on the other side of the car, following after Eddie, who was hot on the trail of his own imposter. After Cheng passed the car, the stranger's form flickered and was replaced by that of Cheng.

"Fuckity fuck!" Julianna spat. *No rats over here, but there sure are snakes.*

Julianna hesitated, looking to where she'd left Knox. Helping him was important, but if there were a bunch of Saverus deceiving the crew on the ground, it wouldn't matter if he found the Tangle Thief or not.

Julianna took a couple of steps back before leaping off the edge of the ship and landing in a crouched position with a *thud*.

Knox remembered the strange euphoria he'd felt the last time he'd been on this ship. His father had taught him that unexplained and sudden feelings were usually a sign of deception. This insight was why he'd had no problem leaving the ship each morning to scour the junkyard for items of use.

It was also why, when Mateo had offered him a place to live, Knox hadn't hesitated to accept. Human contact couldn't be replaced—even by a ship that made its habitants feel strangely happy.

This is almost over, Knox thought, seeing the tile where he'd hidden the Tangle Thief. He couldn't believe that it had all come back around like this. The device that had stolen his father and changed the course of his life now rested only a few feet away. It bothered him that this device was still manipulating every aspect of his life.

But once I hand it over, I'll be free, Knox told himself, kneeling. He dug his fingers into the side of the tile, trying to pry it up.

To his horror, it didn't budge.

Knox stared around. He hid the Tangle Thief under a tile that was two away from the outer wall, and three away from the door to the right.

He stood back and counted again, then he smiled. He'd counted wrong before.

Taking a step forward, Knox squatted down again, this time easily lifting the loose tile out of place. In a small compartment under the ground sat the wooden box that Alleira had given him.

Knox's arms suddenly itched. His stomach tightened.

He took a shallow breath. *Grab it and go,* he told himself.

Knox shook his head, rejecting his inner voice. He needed to ensure that the Tangle Thief was still here.

Lifting the cube-shaped box out of the floor, he let the tile fall back. It made a loud clattering noise that caused him to jump.

He sniffed, running his hand across his nose. His nerves were frayed, but he was fine. He had the Tangle Thief.

Letting out a long breath, Knox lifted the lid off the wooden box and stared down. Nestled inside were three controller-like objects. He reached forward, hesitating briefly before wrapping his hand around one of the pieces. He lifted the client into the air, looking it over.

This was what he'd used to try and find his father. Since its receiver had been destroyed when Cheng used it, the client transported him to the Tangle Thief that lay in the box. The one that Hatch had built.

Running footsteps stole Knox's attention.

He bolted to a standing position, still holding the client. A moment later, Knox's father materialized, halting at the sight of him.

"There you are," Cheng said, his gaze skipping down to the box at Knox's feet. "Is that…?"

"Stay back!" Knox yelled.

"Son?" Cheng asked, looking hurt. "It's me. You don't have to worry. Now, is that the Tangle Thief?"

Knox lifted his pair of goggles to his eyes. Before he could adjust them, his father dove at him, wrapping his hands around his waist and knocking him hard against the wall. Knox's comm fell out of his ear upon impact.

He brought the hand holding the client around hard, knocking his father—or rather, the Saverus pretending to be his father—in the side of the head. Cheng would never attack him; he didn't have a violent bone in his body.

Whoever was on top of Knox was purely evil. The imposter wrapped his hands around Knox's head, lifting it up before knocking his skull hard against the metal below him.

The blinding pain took over, stealing Knox's breath. He let out a long groan.

The form of Cheng jumped off him and darted for the box. Knox rolled around onto his stomach and reached for the Saverus's foot, pulling it off the ground. The Saverus fell to the tile floor, the box tumbling out of its hands, and both remaining pieces bouncing in different directions.

The foot that Knox had just grabbed kicked him in the nose. He heard a crunching noise as searing pain exploded across his face, and Knox knew at once that his nose had been broken. He covered his face with his hands, the blood like a fountain, draining straight into his mouth.

He pushed up to a standing position, knocking into the wall. His eyes were watering so badly he could hardly make out the scene in front of him. Wiping his eyes, he blinked. He couldn't fight or do anything, mostly blind and his nose shattered. When his vision cleared he would have rather seen anything than what he found.

The hallway was empty and the Tangle Thief was gone.

24

Outskirts Junkyard, Planet L2SCQ-6 in Frontier space

Julianna shot the form of Cheng that she'd tracked through the junkyard. A moment after being hit, it morphed into its natural snake form.

"Another Saverus has bitten the dust," Julianna said into the comm.

"Good work. The team is all loaded up," Fletcher announced.

Pip, can you bring the Q-Ships over to our location?

You know I can.

Will you?

Please?

Now.

I'm on it, boss.

"I've just taken down the one who was posing as me," Eddie said. "That fucker was definitely not as handsome though. I hope you didn't fall for his act."

"I used the goggles," Julianna admitted.

"Whatever. Call the ship," Eddie said.

"Copy that," Julianna said.

"Knox, what's your status?" Eddie asked.

There was no reply.

"Knox, are you there?" Julianna asked, sprinting around the battlecruiser, to the open end.

Her attention was suddenly stolen by three chrome transport ships, lifting into the air in the distance. They hovered high up for a moment and then shot forward, speeding for space.

"The Saverus are leaving!" Julianna sang.

"That's a good sign," Eddie said at her back. She turned, offering him a wide smile.

"I wonder why," Julianna said.

Knox materialized on the fifth deck, looking down at them, his face covered in blood.

Julianna shot a look of horror at Eddie, who returned it. "Knox, you have the Tangle Thief?" Julianna asked.

Knox shook his head. "They took it."

Eddie and Julianna used the Saverus goggles on everyone in both Q-Ships before taking off. From the air, Eddie was able to see how much the Saverus cared for their Petigrens. They'd left them all behind. The rats were scurrying among the wreckage and spreading throughout the junkyard.

"The Petigrens are going to take over that poor planet,"

Julianna said over the comm, as her ship hovered next to Eddie's.

"Yeah. Once they breach the borders of the junkyard, there will be no stopping those blood suckers," Eddie said.

"They aren't natural," Fletcher said, an edge to his voice.

"If I may," Hatch imparted from the main ship. "I've been monitoring the situation on the ground, and I might have a solution."

"What's that?" Eddie asked, staring down at the junkyard. He watched as the Petigrens covered the fire tower in the center like a hoard of ants. A moment later, the structure fell to the ground in a cloud of smoke.

"The leveling laser is complete," Hatch said.

"Oh!" Eddie chirped.

"Can we confine the leveling to the junkyard?" Julianna asked.

"Absolutely, I have the settings honed with great precision," Hatch said.

"Because you're a fucking rockstar," Eddie cheered.

"Do you want me to activate it?" Hatch asked, ignoring Eddie, as usual.

"Do we agree that if hundreds of Petigrens are left on this planet, they'll destroy it?" Julianna asked.

"Destroy it and its people, who have already suffered enough," Eddie said emphatically.

"Not to mention that the battlecruiser will finally be destroyed, releasing a lot of the energy it stole," Pip reasoned.

"And preventing it from stealing anymore," Knox agreed.

"Okay, Hatch. Activate the leveling laser," Julianna ordered.

A moment later, the mechanic reported, "Laser has been triggered. It will deploy in three... two... one..."

From where *Ricky Bobby* hung in space, a red laser beam shot down and connected with the junkyard. For a moment, nothing happened. Then the laser beam brightened and expanded, casting everything within the perimeter in red.

Eddie sucked in a breath as a great cloud of dust and smoke shot into the air. When it settled, there was nothing left where the junkyard had been but flat land, covered in ash.

25

Infirmary, *Ricky Bobby*, Tangki System

Knox turned the client over in his hands. He hadn't let the piece go since he first picked it up in the severed battlecruiser. For some reason, holding onto it made him feel better.

His nose had been completely repaired, and the Petigren bite bandaged hours ago, but he still sat on a bed in the infirmary. It felt wrong for him to leave when he still felt so broken.

Eddie and Julianna said that losing the Tangle Thief was their fault—that one of them should have been with him. Cheng had told him that he was proud of him. They'd all tried to convince him that there was nothing else he could have done. After rolling the events around in his head—he had given that fight all he had—Knox had to agree. But after all this time, after everything, losing the Tangle Thief was a brutal blow.

"Are you still in here feeling sorry for yourself?" Hatch asked from the door.

Knox shrugged. "This seemed like the right place for me at the moment."

Hatch's tentacles moved rhythmically as he shuffled into the room. "So we lost the Tangle Thief. So what?"

"How can you say that?"

"Because if it wasn't for you, we would have lost it a long time ago," Hatch stated.

Knox blinked at him, confused.

"The Saverus have been after that device for over ten years," Hatch continued. "If it had been in Area 126, it would already be in their hands. Hell, if you hadn't taken it from your house, they probably would have gotten it a long time ago."

"But they have it now, and that's what we've been fighting against," Knox lamented.

"And we will continue to fight," Hatch countered. "Sometimes you win and sometimes you lose. Today, we had a setback… but do you think that means Ghost Squadron is going to give up?"

Knox shook his head. "I can't imagine Eddie and Julianna ever giving up."

Hatch sort of smiled, a gesture that was rare for the Londil. "Me either. You know, in a way, I think it's better that the Saverus have the Tangle Thief now."

"What? What do you mean?" Knox asked.

"They are up to something, and I have a feeling it's major," Hatch explained. "If we had beaten them to the Tangle Thief, do you think *they'd* give up?"

Knox considered this for a moment. The Saverus wanted the Tangle Thief for a reason, one that was no doubt sinister, knowing what kind of evil race they were.

"No, they'd find another way to accomplish whatever they are up to."

Hatch pointed a tentacle at Knox. "You got it, Gunner. At least this way, they have a device that I know how to track. Once they start operating the Tangle Thief, it's going to set off many red flags."

"But the tears and radiation, they are deadly," Knox stated.

Hatch leaned in closer. "Don't tell anyone, but there are tears and radiation all over the galaxy. They are just in places where they don't affect anything, or we have them under control."

"You're trying to make me feel better," Knox said, giving Hatch an accusatory expression.

"I would never dream of doing such a thing. I'm simply saying that we are in a better place to stop the Saverus, now that we can follow them."

"Yeah, I guess." Knox turned the client over in his hands.

"There's something else that's worth celebrating," Hatch ventured.

Knox looked up, curious. "What's that?"

"This whole journey. You've found your father, recaptured your memories, and found the missing piece of your puzzle." Hatch pointed to the client.

"My puzzle?" Knox asked.

"Son, I've always thought you had a unique talent that

most people in a pool of a million couldn't match. An instinct that could make you possibly the best mechanical engineer of your generation." Hatch cleared his throat, looking down at the client. "But what you've lacked all along isn't something I can teach you, or even give to you... When you hold that client in your hands, what are you thinking about?"

Knox found himself smiling. "It reminds me of how I felt before everything in my life fell apart. When I picked up this client for the first time, I had such confidence that it would bring me back to my father. Fix things."

"And in a way, it did," Hatch said. "It just took a little longer than you expected. But if that Tangle Thief didn't send you on the journey that it did, you might have never found your father again; the Federation might have placed you in a home, and you would have been brought up by a nice family, but there would have been no visit to Planet L2SCQ-6, and certainly no Ghost Squadron."

"So you think the Tangle Thief actually saved my life?" Knox asked.

"I think that it's all about perspective. Two people can look at a situation, and where one sees a tragedy, the other might see a miracle."

Knox nodded, thinking. "Do you think that, when I lost my father and used the Tangle Thief, I lost my confidence?"

"Do you think that?" Hatch fired back at him.

"Yeah, I think it makes sense that I would have lost my nerve then."

"And maybe it changes things now that you have

perspective. Maybe you see that everything turned out for the best and that you made the right decisions," Hatch said.

Knox tilted the client in his hands, noticing how ordinary this complex object was. "So confidence is the one thing I'm lacking that you can't teach me?"

"Confidence is the one thing that we all need in order to be successful at anything," Hatch said, a meaningful expression in his dark eyes.

"You sound like you're speaking from experience," Knox observed.

"Gunner, I've been doing this for a long time, and even I sometimes lose my confidence." Hatch reached out and plucked the client from his hands, holding it up in front of his face. "But the important thing to remember is that no matter what we lose, we can always get it back."

Brig, *Ricky Bobby*, Tangki System

"You requested to see us," Julianna said matter-of-factly.

Eddie threw a contemptuous glare at the Saverus and then said to Julianna, "We have to keep this short. We have more pressing issues to deal with than looking at this snake-piece-of-shit."

The Saverus swayed behind the bars of her cell. "I've been thinking..."

"That you don't want to be thrown out the airlock?" Eddie pretended to ask.

The Saverus shook her giant head. "That you were right. The council has turned their backs on me; my partner put my life at risk. I'm serving the Saverus when they won't do anything to serve me."

"What does that mean?" Julianna pried.

"It means that I'll tell you whatever you want to know. I'll talk," the Saverus said.

"How do we know you won't betray us, like you did before?" Eddie challenged.

"Because I have no reason to," she said.

"You want to live. This could be purely out of self-preservation," Eddie reasoned.

The snake's eyes glowed bright for a moment. "My entire race has betrayed me. Believe me when I say that I've considered death to be a better way out of all of this."

"That's morbid," Eddie stated.

"The truth is that what you said made me think. My race is ruthless and selfish. They know that using the Tangle Thief has major repercussions—Dr. Cheng Sung told us that much—but the elders don't care," the Saverus said.

Eddie glanced at his watch, tapping his foot and ignoring the Saverus. "Jules, can this wait? We've got somewhere to be."

She squinted at him. "If you're throwing me a surprise birthday party, I'm going to kick you in the nuts."

The Saverus laughed, which sounded strange, marked as it was by the hissing. Both Eddie and Julianna gave her sideways looks.

"What?" she asked, sinking back. "That was funny."

Julianna shook her head. "We will consider your offer.

If you talk, we'll keep you alive…but we can't offer you any more than that."

"And we want to know everything," Eddie pressed.

The Saverus nodded. "I'll cooperate. I'll tell you what the Saverus are up to, how they operate, and where the Petigren colonies can be found."

Julianna looked at Eddie, suddenly teeming with quiet excitement. She wanted to stay, question the Saverus. They needed to know as much as possible, and quickly.

However, Eddie tapped his watch, that anxious look in his eyes.

"Okay, fine," Julianna finally said. "We will return tomorrow to learn everything you have to offer," she assured the prisoner.

Eddie strode for the door and pulled it open. Again, he tapped his foot.

"Oh, and one more thing," the Saverus said.

Julianna cast a quick glance over her shoulder, her facial expression saying, *'What?'*

"My name is Penrae," the Saverus said.

———

"We lost the battle, but we have a great advantage now," Julianna said, her tone urgent.

She hadn't stopped talking since they left the brig.

"Right, right." Eddie ran his hands absentmindedly over his stubbled chin.

"If we can take out the Petigren colonies, that's their

brute force. The Saverus will be mostly powerless," Julianna continued.

Eddie halted in front of a door, holding a hand up to pause Julianna. "Can we put that Saverus business aside for a moment?"

Julianna's mouth popped open like she was going to argue. She nodded, seeming to resign a bit.

"Good," Eddie chirped. "Now, I realize that, with the mission, you've been distracted. And, I know I give you a ton of shit for risking your life for things I deem silly, but I want to take a moment to commend you. Jules, you're the most stubborn person I've ever worked with. You're a control freak at times, and you drive me downright fucking bonkers."

"Please tell me this is going somewhere, or I really will kick you in the balls," Julianna said.

Eddie turned the handle for the door, but kept it closed. "Yes. My point is that I wouldn't have you any other way. I may not always understand you, but when all is said and done, you've never let me down. You've never let *any* of us down. You, Commander Fregin, are fucking amazing."

Eddie stepped back as he opened the door, throwing his arm out in presentation.

Standing squarely in the middle of the room was a dog that looked almost like Harley. It was Harley, but...he was bigger, his brown coat was sleeker. When Julianna stepped into the room, Harley stood at attention, his ears perking up.

Julianna blinked down at the beautiful, almost regal dog. She tilted her head to the side, trying to compute all the emotions that were piling up one on top of the other inside her.

Eddie's words. The fact that Harley had made it. Everything that had happened. All stirred together, it made something in her chest thump hard. Julianna found herself smiling down at the dog. His bright eyes seemed to smile back.

Hello, Julianna, Harley said in her head.

Hello, Harley, she said, a little unnerved.

Thank you for saving me...again.

I did what I felt was right.

Harley stood, gracefully strolled over to Julianna, twirled around, and sat down dutifully at her feet.

Well, staying by your side feels like the right thing for me to do, he said, looking up at her with deep loyalty shining in his eyes.

FINIS

I work a lot. Craig Martelle writes a book in the time it takes me to clean my downstairs half-bathroom. He's a machine who reports to work eighty-hours a week. I don't think I work that many hours, but I'm also a full-time mom to a six-year old. I work as much as makes sense to get the books written, which usually leaves me with little time to socialize, which isn't a problem for me since I have friends in my head. But my "real" friends, who don't fly Q-Ships and have badass super powers, have communicated a concern that I don't spend enough time partying. Well, I have *one* friend in particular.

Just before I was about to start this book, *this friend*, who I'm glad doesn't do illegal drugs, because she's very pushy, demanded that I go on a three-day cruise to Mexico. Let's cut this long story short. I went. I got the drink package. The cruiseline made money on the drink package. I tried to pretend I was doing research for my next book by strolling around a giant cruiseship, which I reasoned was pretty much the same thing as a spaceship. I think my reasoning was faulty, but I obviously should have drank more tequila. That's going to be the moral to this story when I get to the end. Damn that drink package!

I've now entitled that cruise the "Great Reset". You know those times in your life where everything goes completely wrong so that everything can go completely right? I know, that probably doesn't make sense, but it's true. I found myself sharing a closet of a room with two other women and a forced feeling that I needed to "party and relax." The cruise started off badly and got worse as we sailed out to sea.

Why, you ask? Yes, probably because I didn't take advantage of my drink package.

But also, because my life was resetting itself. Being a full-time author is tough. It's demanding and scary and I'm constantly putting my ego in the corner. Balancing time for friends is hard and I guilt myself for not spending more time with people. And most importantly, there's my daughter. I could go back into the steady profession of college administration, but that sucked out my soul. When I tell Lydia to follow her dreams and take risks, I want her to see I'm talking the talk and walking the walk.

So I went on this trip conflicted on if I was doing the right thing being a writer. Was that the best thing for me, my daughter and my loved ones? I returned to the west coast after having a miserable time and there were two things I had missed dearly: Lydia and writing.

Michael and I had a nice heart to heart during the construction of this book. I'm sure many of you know this, but MA really cares about the wellbeing of the authors he works with, not just about the books. We discussed this "reset" I was going through and afterwards, I felt infinitely better. Following our dreams is tough. It's scary. It's demanding. But I've got a fantastic team and people like Michael and Craig to support my efforts.

If I hadn't gone on that cruise then I wouldn't have questioned my current job as an author. I wouldn't have realized that it's the only thing that truly makes me happy professionally. I wouldn't have faced up to all my fears and realized, no matter what, I want to make this work.

I also wouldn't have realized that I have the perfect profession because I never feel that I need a break from it. My friend demanded that I take a vacation, but when I returned, I realized I didn't want one. I had missed my job.

So I have the perfect job for me. I have an amazing child. I have *some* time for other people and things. Fuck anyone who doesn't like it.

Okay. I'm done with that. Moving on.

I love interacting with the fans on Facebook. My editor might have thought I'd lost my mind when I told her that I was throwing in a bunch of random references because I was challenged by the readers. Otter assassins and trash pandas in a sci-fi book isn't something you see every day. So I've got a lot of thanks to give to the fans for the suggestions for this book. If I miss anyone, please message Craig (preferably at an off hour).

John Calvert, you're the mastermind behind this whole otter assassin business. I blame you for the rubber chickens as well as Rocco Lauria, Liz Ehret Re, Tracey Brynes,

Wayne Hamilton, Ron Gailey, Sherry Foster, Kevin Mcdonnell, Pat O'Brien. Chrisa Changala, not only did you educate me on terms, but I loved throwing in the trash panda reference. This whole thread on Facebook kept me laughing today. Like Kristoffer Pyle's giraffe. That shit was genius.

I also polled the fans for suggestions for the karaoke scene. I couldn't believe how many times Bohemian Rhapsody was mentioned. Thanks to Tim Adams, Mandi Fawcett and Karen Cabael for that. Natale Roberts suggestion of Hey Jude was randomly picked as Chester's song. I had to include Lori Hendriks for I Don't Want to Miss a Thing. Oh and Eric Hernandez, thanks for the suggestion for Thunderstruck. You all rock. I added all the suggestions to the playlist for Ghost Squadron.

Ron Gailey, I love your suggestions. Never stop sending them. The laser that blasts the junkyard at the end was one of your ideas that I ran with. Thank you.

Cars again played a big role in the book. I actually got bored of spaceships and guns on the cover so I told my cover designer to add a classic car. I used many of the suggestions from the readers for cars mentioned in the book. Thanks to Alastar Wilson for the '69 Corvette Stingray idea. Diane L. Smith gets the credit for the Mustang 390GT. David Pollard and Nora McGuirk also gave me great suggestions for the 67 GTO and many other cars. Thank you all!

Okay, without further ado, I turn the stage over to MA and his tap shoes.

Check out Sarah Noffke's Paranormal Thriller:

Ren Series:

Get it here

He is the most powerful man to ever live, and therefore doomed to misery.

Born with the power to control minds, hypnotize others, and read thoughts, Ren Lewis, is certain of one thing: God made a mistake. No one should be born with so much power. A monster awoke in him the same year he received his gifts.

At ten years old. A prepubescent boy with the ability to control others might merely abuse his powers, but Ren allowed it to corrupt him. And since he can have and do anything he wants, Ren should be happy. However, his journey teaches him that harboring so much power doesn't bring happiness, it steals it.

Once this realization sets in, Ren makes up his mind to do the one thing that can bring his tortured soul some peace. He must kill the monster.

Read Ren: The Man Behind the Monster.

(THANK YOU for reading these notes... That is all!)

<Tappity tappity tappity tap.>

No, I can't really just say that and leave but I was tempted, so sorely tempted.

Who the hell is going to surpass the baring of someone's soul like Sarah just did?

I know I can't.

It feels like those books where I was author blocked by Martha Carr and Brandon Barr. They shared these deep and intimate hard times in their lives in up on stage (in their author notes), and then the light switches from them (with the accompanying applause) to me and I'm there, eyes wide open, staring at Martha and Brandon then staring at the crowd thinking....*shit!*

<Tappity tappity tappity tap!>

I enjoyed my conversation with Sarah and really appreciate her offering me a chance to see inside her mind and feelings. She mentioned a situation with her brother I will carry with me the rest of my life. She said this:

When my brother died, he died with songs inside him we will never hear...

That was a mic-drop moment for me.

I'm honored to be entrusted with her work, her dreams, her aspirations and above all, her friendship.

Let's make sure your stories are all on (digital) paper, Sarah.

Ad Aeternitatem,
Michael Anderle

(P.S. – I laughed out loud and pumped my fist in the air when she said in her author notes, "If I miss anyone, please message Craig (preferably at an off hour)."

Absolutely, please do that.

It will be fucking hilarious – I promise. That jerk made me a horrible mayor in one of his books and I've yet to get him back for that.

(Not that I'm bitter or anything.)

ACKNOWLEDGMENTS

Sarah Noffke

Thank you to Michael Anderle for taking my calls and allowing me to play in this universe. It's been a blast since the beginning.

Thank you to Craig Martelle for cheering for me. I've learned so much working with you. This wild ride just keeps going and going.

Thank you to Jen, Tim, Steve, Andrew and Jeff for all the work on the books, covers and championing so much of the publishing.

Thank you to our beta team. I can't believe how fast you all can turn around books. The JIT team sometimes scares me, but usually just with how impressively knowledgeable they are.

Thank you to our amazing readers. I asked myself a question the other day and it had a strange answer. I asked if I would still write if trapped on a desert island and no one would ever read the books. The answer was yes, but the feeling connected to it was different. It wouldn't be as much fun to write if there wasn't awesome readers to share it with. Thank you.

Thank you to my friends and family for all the support and love.

Sarah Noffke, an Amazon Best Seller, writes YA and NA sci-fi fantasy, paranormal and urban fantasy. She is the author of the Lucidites, Reverians, Ren, Vagabond Circus, Olento Research and Soul Stone Mage series. Noffke holds a Masters of Management and teaches college business courses. Most of her students have no idea that she toils away her hours crafting fictional characters. Noffke's books are top rated and best-sellers on Kindle. Currently, she has eighteen novels published. Her books are available in paperback, audio and in Spanish, Portuguese and Italian. http://www.sarahnoffke.com

Check out other work by this author here.

The Soul Stone Mage Series:
House of Enchanted #1:
The Kingdom of Virgo has lived in peace for thousands of years...until now.

The humans from Terran have always been real

assholes to the witches of Virgo. Now a silent war is brewing, and the timing couldn't be worse. Princess Azure will soon be crowned queen of the Kingdom of Virgo.

In the Dark Forest a powerful potion-maker has been murdered.

Charmsgood was the only wizard who could stop a deadly virus plaguing Virgo. He also knew about the devastation the people from Terran had done to the forest.

Azure must protect her people. Mend the Dark Forest. Create alliances with savage beasts. No biggie, right?

But on coronation day everything changes. Princess Azure isn't who she thought she was and that's a big freaking problem.

Welcome to The Revelations of Oriceran. Check out the entire series here.

The Lucidites Series:

Awoken, #1:

Around the world humans are hallucinating after sleepless nights.

In a sterile, underground institute the forecasters keep reporting the same events.

And in the backwoods of Texas, a sixteen-year-old girl is about to be caught up in a fierce, ethereal battle.

Meet Roya Stark. She drowns every night in her dreams, spends her hours reading classic literature to avoid her family's ridicule, and is prone to premonitions—which are becoming more frequent. And now her dreams are filled with strangers offering to reveal what she has always wanted to know: Who is she? That's the question that haunts her, and she's about to find out. But will Roya live to regret learning the truth?

***Stunned**, #2*

***Revived**, #3*

The Reverians Series:

***Defects**, #1*:

In the happy, clean community of Austin Valley, everything appears to be perfect. Seventeen-year-old Em Fuller, however, fears something is askew. Em is one of the new generation of Dream Travelers. For some reason, the gods have not seen fit to gift all of them with their expected special abilities. Em is a Defect—one of the unfortunate Dream Travelers not gifted with a psychic power. Desperate to do whatever it takes to earn her gift, she endures painful daily injections along with commands from her overbearing, loveless father. One of the few bright spots in her life is the return of a friend she had thought dead—but with his return comes the knowledge of a shocking, unforgivable truth. The society Em thought was protecting her has actually been betraying her, but she has no idea how to break away from its authority without hurting everyone she loves.

***Rebels**, #2*

***Warriors**, #3*

Vagabond Circus Series:

***Suspended**, #1*:

When a stranger joins the cast of Vagabond Circus—a circus that is run by Dream Travelers and features real magic—mysterious events start happening. The once orderly grounds of the circus become riddled with hidden threats. And the ringmaster realizes not only are his circus and its magic at risk, but also his very life.

Vagabond Circus caters to the skeptics. Without skeptics, it would close its doors. This is because Vagabond Circus runs for two reasons and only two reasons: first and foremost to provide the lost and lonely Dream Travelers a place to be illustrious. And secondly, to show the nonbelievers that there's still magic in the world. If they believe, then they care, and if they care, then they don't destroy. They stop the small abuse that day-by-day breaks down humanity's spirit. If Vagabond Circus makes one skeptic believe in magic, then they halt the cycle, just a little bit. They allow a little more love into this world. That's Dr. Dave Raydon's mission. And that's why this ringmaster recruits. That's why he directs. That's why he puts on a show that makes people question their beliefs. He wants the world to believe in magic once again.

Paralyzed, #2
Released, #3

Ren Series:
Ren: The Man Behind the Monster, #1:
Born with the power to control minds, hypnotize others, and read thoughts, Ren Lewis, is certain of one thing: God made a mistake. No one should be born with so much power. A monster awoke in him the same year he received his gifts. At ten years old. A prepubescent boy with the ability to control others might merely abuse his

powers, but Ren allowed it to corrupt him. And since he can have and do anything he wants, Ren should be happy. However, his journey teaches him that harboring so much power doesn't bring happiness, it steals it. Once this realization sets in, Ren makes up his mind to do the one thing that can bring his tortured soul some peace. He must kill the monster.

Note This book is NA and has strong language, violence and sexual references.

Ren: God's Little Monster, #2
Ren: The Monster Inside the Monster, #3
Ren: The Monster's Adventure, #3.5
Ren: The Monster's Death

Olento Research Series:

Alpha Wolf, #1:

Twelve men went missing.

Six months later they awake from drug-induced stupors to find themselves locked in a lab.

And on the night of a new moon, eleven of those men, possessed by new—and inhuman—powers, break out of their prison and race through the streets of Los Angeles until they disappear one by one into the night.

Olento Research wants its experiments back. Its CEO, Mika Lenna, will tear every city apart until he has his werewolves imprisoned once again. He didn't undertake a huge risk just to lose his would-be assassins.

However, the Lucidite Institute's main mission is to save the world from injustices. Now, it's Adelaide's job to find these mutated men and protect them and society, and fast. Already around the nation, wolflike men are being spotted. Attacks on innocent women are happening. And then, Adelaide realizes what her next step must be: She has to find the alpha wolf first. Only once she's located him can she stop whoever is behind this experiment to create wild beasts out of human beings.

Lone Wolf, #2

    Rabid Wolf, #3

    Bad Wolf, #4

CONNECT WITH THE AUTHORS

Michael Anderle Social

Website:
http://kurtherianbooks.com/

Email List:
http://kurtherianbooks.com/email-list/

Facebook Here:
https://www.
facebook.com/TheKurtherianGambitBooks/